American Antigone

American Antigone

Matthew Archbold

RESOURCE *Publications* • Eugene, Oregon

AMERICAN ANTIGONE

Resource Publications
An Imprint of Wipf and Stock Publishers
199 W. 8th Ave., Suite 3
Eugene, OR 97401

www.wipfandstock.com

PAPERBACK ISBN: 978-1-7252-8272-8
HARDCOVER ISBN: 978-1-7252-8273-5
EBOOK ISBN: 978-1-7252-8274-2

Manufactured in the U.S.A.   09/04/20

1

THUDD!

A world-changing crash shook Susan Doyle.

The sound that a 208-pound man makes when falling without so much as holding out his arms thundered throughout the hotel room, followed by the tinkling of two pens and a reading lamp elevating briefly off the desk and clinking back down.

Susan felt the reverberation in her toes through the carpeted floorboards before even comprehending the sound.

Silence.

Seated on the edge of the hotel bed, Susan sought to stabilize her shaking by clutching the red jagged-patterned hotel blanket in her fists. Nearly out of frame, she stared wide eyed into the smudged black-framed mirror on the wall across from the bed.

It wasn't her explicit thought that nothing would change if she remained still, but she stared at her bisected self as if that were true.

"Edwaaaard?" Her thin voice cracked and faltered as she called out to the other room. She thought her voice sounded alone the way a voice sometimes can.

Silence. Well, not silence; merely the absence of voices. The clang of the heater under the window, the snarl of passing traffic twelve stories down, the high-pitched shriek of pipes behind the wall from cold showers taken by indifferent strangers whose lives hadn't just changed forever. Those sounds were so expected and constant that sometimes they blended into what we call silence, the impersonal noise of people and things we don't know or understand.

"Edwaaaard?"

She hated that her voice sounded like a little girl's. Trembling. Weak. Unconsciously, she pulled a strand of her shoulder-length blond hair tightly

1

across her lip. She didn't expect an answer, but she called out again anyway, this time trying to make her voice more authoritative, commanding.

"Edwwaaaaaard. Pleeeeeeeeease?"

She failed.

Just moments before, he'd stood before her promising to care for their child. He'd said it to make her feel better, and she pretended to believe him to prevent his worrying about the pregnancy test on the mattress.

They'd embraced, him standing at the foot of the bed in his T-shirt and boxer shorts and she sitting in a white robe, her face pressed into his chest. He'd said they could stay in that room for months, order in. They wouldn't even need clothes, and only after they got tired of looking at the same four walls would they even consider venturing out into the cruel, slapping world.

Susan had taken comfort in that imaginary world even as she thought about Edward's wife and children three thousand miles away in Pennsylvania. Despite all the concern and worry, she also believed she saw a small but undeniable stirring of joy in his face. Yes, a seed of joy had threatened to kick. A child. A new start.

But all that was gone now.

Alone and scared, she dialed 911.

2

WHEN SUSAN OPENED THE door, she squinted in the light from the hallway. She stepped back as the EMTs hurried in with surgical precision, pulling out their flashlights, kneeling next to the figure on the floor, and checking for a pulse.

The San Francisco medical examiner later concluded District Attorney Edward Prince might have survived the embolism with significant brain damage, but the fall itself proved instantly fatal.

Susan watched them glance gravely at each other. She lowered herself to the edge of the desk chair and stared into the bedroom.

As the activity subsided, two police officers spoke to Susan with deliberate calm, writing down the details she provided. Sometimes she spoke with her hand over her mouth as if she were telling secrets and explained that Mr. Prince had traveled to California for a political fundraiser. Technically, it was a fundraiser for several Republican candidates, but Prince was the star attraction—a Republican leading in the polls in a purple state. Susan also informed them in a whisper that Mr. Prince's wife and two children needed to be notified of . . . his condition. When she called him "Mr. Prince," the two officers glanced at each other. One smirked, but Susan pretended not to notice.

As the EMTs waited for the medical examiner, Susan walked to the corner of the bedroom, turned her face toward the window, and dialed the Thebes county chair of the Republican Party, Frank Whipple. He received the news as if it were a change in a business project. He actually said, "Okie dokie." *Holy crap,* she thought. *He actually said, "Okie dokie."* She just tried to keep her voice from cracking until she hung up.

She returned to the doorway of the main room. The detectives, the medical examiner, three uniformed officers, two EMTs, the hotel manager, and the coroner all crowded into the living room, speaking in hushed tones while the body of the man she . . . adored (Admired? Loved?) lay on the ground, arms twisted at odd angles. And Edward's eyes, fixed on nothing. But they weren't Edward's eyes any longer; the color had already drained out of them.

A uniformed officer whispered, and the others stifled laughter and looked guiltily toward her before springing back to their duties. She wondered if to perform their jobs they had to turn off part of their humanity, like a tourniquet allowed one part of the body to die to save the rest.

At some point one of the first responders texted an editor of the *San Francisco Reporter* named Tom Robicheaux, who wrote down the name "Edward Prince" on a purple Post-it note, googled the name, bounded from his desk, and took the stairs down to the "dungeon" two at a time.

The death of Edward Prince, father of two daughters and husband to Emily, was a dreadful shock for those who knew him. But for those who never knew him, the longtime district attorney and Senate candidate from Pennsylvania found dead in his underwear in a hotel with a female employee was national news.

3

Paul Barnes stared at his blank computer screen. He had no idea what to write. He was in trouble. He'd been warned it was the last straw two straws ago.

Paul's big story the previous month had been a misfire. He'd reported on a computer engineering club at Loyola Marymount University that had predicted that due to an increase in solar flares emitting high-energy radiation, Earth's magnetic field would expand, and a low-orbiting non-functional satellite would get yanked out of orbit and dragged back to Earth, where it would crash and cause untold damage. However, after running the story, he discovered the students were actually running an experiment for psychology class about the effect of phony science stories on the populace.

Soooo . . . since then things hadn't been going well.

Reporters at the *San Francisco Reporter* were responsible for two stories per day, ten a week. Paul had only three planned for the entire week, so he kept an eye on the stairs, expecting a visit from the editorial comeuppance department.

When he began working there just two years before, he'd been responsible for merely one story per day. Since then, the number of reporters had been cut in half, so it was a matter of simple mathematics.

Most of his stories were rewritten press releases or borrowed ideas from Twitter with some colorful quotes and half-clever turns of phrase, but some still induced a bit of pride. Some. A few.

The reporters often huddled in a cubicle and commiserated about the "churnalism" they were forced to practice and the awful antics of their editor, "Nanzi," whose actual name was Nancy but whose quick-to-anger personality, unremitting attention to detail, and lack of any vestige of mercy made the nickname easy. One of the older editors who'd recently been nudged (Shoved? Heaved?) into retirement once confided to Paul that

Nancy had been a sweet kid, but after being promoted, she found it awkward to manage her friends, so she emotionally distanced herself. Ten years later, reporters merely feared her.

Sometimes the dungeon dwellers shared how idealistically they'd begun and how thrilled they'd been to work in a newsroom with Pulitzer banners hanging from the ceiling. But the last banner had been hung nine years before.

None of them had experience with another large city paper, but they were certain that others operated more professionally. Eventually, they resigned themselves that if the editors were just using them for maximum labor at minimum pay, they should use them in return to build their resumes and bounce to a nice cushy editor's job somewhere else. They often delighted in imagining the look on Nanzi's face when they all abandoned ship on the same day.

When Paul arrived at work, he walked down the "the staircase of shame" in the back to avoid Nanzi's notice. The email he'd sent contained three of the most yawn-inducing story ideas destined for the "Suburban" section or worse yet, "Lifestyle." He also implied some vague leads on other possible stories, but he suspected that no matter how he massaged the language, his email would incite the rage beast upstairs, who would dispatch her eager assistant, Tom Robicheaux, to fetch her prey.

Few respected Robicheaux. They viewed him as a human space filler, the equivalent of the sound someone made when clearing their throat or saying "um" or "y' know" while deciding what to say next.

Three months prior, a highly respected editor accepted a job in New York, so the paper promoted Robicheaux from underperforming and lazy copy editor to incompetent and disrespected assistant night editor while they secretly collected resumes for a permanent replacement to banish him back to copy editing.

Robicheaux still attempted to retain friendships with reporters, so when he emerged from the stairwell, Paul questioned whether he had come to make chitchat or to politely escort Paul upstairs where Nanzi would tear him from sternum to sphincter and say something along the lines of how he'd failed to live up to her expectations or he had turned out to be less than intended. That was how she spoke. One time she told a reporter that she found his presence "inconvenient."

Reporters could easily track Robicheaux's "messy on purpose" dirty-brown hair just above the sea of cubicle partitions moving like a shark fin.

Paul watched the fin weave through the sea of cubicles, sometimes stopping for a brief high-pitched squawk with another reporter but always on his way to his ultimate goal—Paul. Everyone in the basement had a Robicheaux imitation. They'd mess their hair, perch a pencil above their ear, and screech insults.

The week before, Robicheaux had made a reporter cry and was ordered to have a sit-down with Human Resources. He told Paul later in confidence (after a fourth beer) that it was worth it because he needed to be thought of as the editor who made reporters cry.

"You on deadline, Community College?" Robicheaux asked as he burst into Paul's burlap cubicle cage. He called Paul that because virtually all the other reporters at the paper had graduated from Ivy League institutions, and Paul had been stupid enough (after seven beers) to admit it bothered him that whenever someone learned he graduated from Penn State, an immediate "less than" symbol appeared in their eyes.

Paul had been hired by the paper two years before through a program whose official reason for being was searching out "undiscovered talent." In truth, due to declining circulation and budgets, the paper was hiring journalists from lesser universities. Paul had been the first. To other reporters, his very existence was an avatar of decay, along with the empty cubicles and dusty banners.

"Oh wait," Robicheaux said loudly, enjoying himself, "you can't be on deadline because you don't have any actual stories this week."

During Paul's first two months at the paper, Robicheaux had sat one cubicle over from Paul. He suspected the editor saw himself as his mentor, which was fine because sometimes it made Paul's life a little easier. Robicheaux pulled at a tear in the burlap, elongating it. He placed his foot on the corner of Paul's desk as if barring his escape. "One story or two short is forgivable," he said, his incisors extending over his bottom lip in a sneer. "But seven missing stories? Seven?"

"I'm leaving myself open to breaking news," Paul replied with a feigned grin (too wide?).

"Interesting excuse," Robicheaux said, still speaking loudly. "Try that one with Nancy, who sees you as a defective, whining millennial drone."

"Well, thanks for cheering me up," Paul said, turning back to his laptop.

"Actually, I come bearing gifts," Robicheaux whispered, then knelt down next to Paul. Paul thought it interesting that Robicheaux bellowed his insults but whispered his kindnesses. "I've got an unresponsive male for you."

"Aren't all males unresponsive?" Paul joked, spinning his chair toward him.

"My former fiancée would agree, but this particular unresponsive male at the Williston Hotel is a Senate candidate from your old neck of the woods in Pennsylvania."

"What's his name?" Paul asked. He reached for Robicheaux's phone, but he held it out of reach above his own head, enjoying having sole possession of the knowledge for a moment longer.

Robicheaux looked at the Post-it between his fingers. "Edward Prince, Thebes County DA."

"Whoa. I know that guy," Paul said. "I went to school with his daughter—daughters, actually . Wait, does anyone else have this story?"

"The body is so fresh, he hasn't even crapped himself yet," Robicheaux replied.

"Great," Paul said, tossing his pad, laptop, and pens into his bag.

"Ah, I tell you someone died and you say 'great,'" Robicheaux said. "I think that's why we get along. Oh, and one more piece of info that might interest you . . . he was found in the hotel room of his lovely assistant."

"Seriously?"

"In his tighty whities," Robicheaux said, smiling.

Paul laughed. "This just gets better and better."

"Any time you're in the doghouse, just howl for me."

Paul dashed up the front stairs, past the editors, and out the door.

After interviewing the EMTs and snapping a pic of the body with his phone from the hallway, Paul approached Susan Doyle, seated alone on the edge of a couch in the hotel lobby. At least he figured it was her. He had seen her picture on the county's website as the first assistant district attorney. Hardly a glamour shot, it showed her standing awkwardly with a briefcase in her right hand and giving a "I'm too busy to fully smile, but if I try really hard I can maybe lift one side of my mouth and stand still for a second" look on her face.

Paul compared it to the woman hunched over on the couch in the lobby. Tall, blond, late twenties. Instead of confident and busy, she was mourning and lost. But it was her. Susan Doyle looked up as Paul approached and cringed as if in expectation of the next horror.

"Hey, I'm Paul Barnes with the San Francisco Reporter. Sorry for your loss, but I have a few questions. Were you out here for a fundraiser?"

She looked down as if Paul would leave if she ignored him.

"Were you and Mr. Prince sharing a room? Did you pay for the hotel room or did the campaign pay? Are you on the campaign staff? Because I didn't see your name on the website."

People looked toward them. Susan scanned the lobby for an escape, stood, and bounded toward the front exit, her heels clicking on the tile. Paul continued apace, peppering her with questions. "I noticed you only rented one room from the hotel. Were you and Mr. Prince staying together?"

Realizing that heading outside would do her no good, she turned toward the women's bathroom. Fearing she'd disappear inside, Paul shot one last volley just as she reached the door. "Why was Mr. Prince in his underwear in your hotel room?"

She pushed on the bathroom door to escape, but the door wouldn't open. She stepped into it, but it didn't budge. Locked. Trapped.

"Ma'am, were you two having an affair?" Paul asked. "Did he have any last words?" Paul hoped one of his questions would provoke a response, something he could use. "Did you—"

"Please, please . . ." she murmured, lowering her head. "Please."

"Ms. Doyle, I'm just trying to get your side of the story."

"Please."

He left her there. It didn't matter. He had the story. He wrote that she had refused to comment.

Three hours later, he returned with a front-page story (below the fold). He fought hard to mention "underwear" up high in the story. Spoiler alert—he couldn't.

The editors decided on "Senate Candidate Found Dead" as the headline" with "No Foul Play Suspected" as the sub. The ensuing paragraphs detailed that Prince likely died from natural causes, but forensic pathologists would perform an autopsy. The story also included speculation about the political ramifications, Prince's criminal prosecution of his own father, which had made him something of a local legend, and questions over who the county would appoint as the new DA.

In the ninth paragraph, Frank Whipple, chair of the Republican Party, explained that Prince had merely been dropping off some files at twenty-seven-year-old Assistant District Attorney Susan Doyle's hotel room when he passed away.

"In his underwear?" Paul had asked, but Whipple referred back to his statement.

After handing in the story, Paul walked down the main stairs past the editors on his way out. Nanzi stopped him. "Hey, great job today." Then she raised her voice, speaking to everyone. "See? You don't need an Ivy League degree. Just some scrappy old-school legwork."

Hearing that credit was being given, Robicheaux poked his head out over his computer. "I actually gave him the tip from an old source of mine."

Ugh. Couldn't he just let Paul have this one? Paul turned to him. "Oh, Tom, you inaccurately described the woman in the room as his assistant. She's actually the assistant district attorney."

Gut punch! Robicheaux blushed as Nancy twisted her face in disgust. Paul just added misogynist to the list of reasons that editors didn't like Robicheaux.

As Paul walked out, a group of copy editors vaping near the door said, "Great job" and "Nice work," but Paul hardly acknowledged them. When he walked out into the parking lot, he inhaled deeply and closed his eyes. Trees and un-mowed grass used to separate the building from the road, but the company had extended the parking lot after renting out a wing of the building to an Internet advertising company. Since then the trees had been shorn into a row of stunted stumps extending out of the grass like rigid fingers bursting from the earth in some B-grade horror movie. A gust of wind blasted his face, but nothing moved.

"Paul!" Nancy startled him by calling him from behind. "The publisher loves this story. He wants a deep-dive follow-up into this guy's life. Get all the dirt."

Paul nodded.

She told him it would take a few days for the medical examiner to rule out homicide and ship the body back to Pennsylvania. She tilted her head as if preparing to ask him if he was alright. Instead, she issued a warning. "Paul, this story is a big deal. Don't mess it up." With that, she closed the door.

He didn't know how to feel. Thrilled? Grateful? Proud? They all were smiles and high fives for the defective millennial drone. Yay! But Paul felt empty. And dammit, he resented feeling that way on what should have been a great night, so he allowed his anger to fill the void. This story would show all his sneering Ivy League coworkers that he was as good as, no, better than them.

He searched the overcast night sky for stars, but only the ever-present synthetic urban dawn filled the horizon. For the first time that day, he thought of Edward Prince's daughters, Anne and Izzy, and how they'd lost their father. He got in his car and turned up the radio.

Comments in the *San Francisco Reporter*.

1. This guy was sort of a local legend. He prosecuted his own father once. Righteous dude. Sorry he's gone.

2. Not too long ago, man sought shelter from the cold and rain. We escaped the terrible plagues, and now man can send his thoughts across the globe quicker than the wind to civilizations ruled by law. We have tamed the earth and bent creation to our will, but from death alone we will find no rescue

3. Typical Republican!

4. I work from home and earn $3,000 a month. Click this link to find out how.

5. This poor family!

6. Don't make this a Republican/Democrat thing. That's crazy. Weakness is human nature. Why must everything be partisan? Stop it. Nothing good will come of that.

7. How the mighty have fallen. Only God himself can show us what he wills in his own way.

4

The Prince girls were high school royalty—admired, imitated, and resented.

Paul didn't know Anne Prince. Not really. He'd been friends with her sister, Izzy. Friendly, anyway. In the same friend group. They were in the same class. Three quarters of the guys were in love with Izzy, and she spoke to all of them as if they were best friends. It wasn't phony. She saw everyone as her friend.

Izzy was tall with wild red hair and green eyes. Though never considered the "popular girl," just about everyone liked her. Anyone who has spent a week in high school understands the difference between "liked" and "popular." She performed in all the school musicals and soaked up all the attention and adoration. She was talented, so it wasn't as if everyone lied about her performance.

Izzy's sister, Anne, wouldn't necessarily be classified as pretty; more like a statue of a beautiful person, a statue behind a rope that people could admire but never approach. Her dark hair fell over her blue eyes. It wasn't that she was abrupt with people, but she always seemed to be on her way somewhere else, and she didn't mind seeming smart in class.

Sometimes Izzy rolled her eyes when someone mentioned her sister or complained offhandedly, not to Paul directly but to others. No great revelation. A teenage girl complained about her older sister. #newsflash

Anne was just one year older than Paul, but a year apart in high school was like being in traffic next to someone else's car. They were on the same road and seeing the same scenery, but there was little communication, and in the long run they were probably going different places.

Paul spoke to Anne for the first time when Izzy told him to meet at her house, so they could head to the park for a group science project. He arrived on his bike at the Princes' house at the end of a cul-de-sac before the other members of the group. He didn't want them to know he had ridden his bike, so he hid it on the side of their house behind a bush and hurried around to the front because it would be weird if somebody saw him.

Anne answered the door. Ready for Izzy's manic energy, Anne's presence unsettled him. Supposedly brilliant, Anne ran just about every committee in high school, and, oh yeah, she was a star athlete too. Not as tall as Izzy but stronger. Her blue eyes pierced. Normally, her black hair fell to her shoulders, but that day she wore it in a ponytail.

"I'm nooooooot readyyyyyyyyyyyyy!" Izzy yodeled from upstairs.

Anne laughed. "She literally just got off the couch when you rang the doorbell, so she'll be a minute."

"It's just a group science project," Paul said. "Why does she need to get ready?"

"Oh, you're a boy," Anne said, shaking her head. "I forgot."

Anne walked into the living room and waved for him to follow. She offered him sweet tea or water, but he declined. She sat on the love seat and pointed him to the couch.

"Soooo, you're Paul, right?" she asked, her legs curled under her.

"Yes." Her knowing his name thrilled and confused him.

"So, how did you two get picked for the group?" Anne asked.

"Oh, everyone wants to be her project partner, but Izzy always picks me," he said. "She thinks I get good grades."

"Do you?"

"Sometimes. Yeah, usually, but she's really smart too even though . . ."

"What?"

"I don't know. I get the idea she doesn't want everyone to know she's smart," he said, then immediately questioned if he'd gone too far.

She smiled, and he exhaled. Seeing Anne in a T-shirt and shorts was strange. In school she seemed so put together, so adult, walking the halls with an intimidating stride, but sitting across from him she seemed like a . . . well, like a girl.

"Borrowing your red shirt, Anne," Izzy called down. "Knew you wouldn't miiiiiind."

Anne smiled.

Anne's shirt said, "Belmont Abbey College," so Paul, desperate for conversation, asked if she planned on attending college there.

"I think so, but I'm not sure. I don't know," she answered, raising her hands to the side of her head. "Aaaaah!" she screamed quietly. "Listen, treasure tenth grade before this huuuuuge life-changing decision that will not only impact the rest of your life but also your family's is thrust upon you."

"Maybe just make your college decision by flipping a coin," Paul suggested, smiling his most charming smile, thankful he'd just gotten his braces removed.

"Hmmm," she pretended to be impressed by the wisdom of this idea. "You've tried this strategy before, and it worked out?"

"Well, 'worked out' is a bit high of a bar, but it's worth a try." Paul congratulated himself internally on his charm as she laughed. "Do you know what you want to major in?".

"OK, Paul," she said, leaning forward in faux confidentiality. "This is our first conversation, but I feel like I can be honest with you."

"I feel the same," he said, adopting her conspiratorial whisper.

"You are the worst conversationalist in the world," she said as if she were delivering terrible medical news. "When speaking with someone, you don't want to bring up the subject they're trying to avoid."

"And I always thought I possessed a gift for conversation," he said. "This is distressing."

"I'm here for you," she said.

They stared at each other for a moment until Paul looked away. When he met Anne's eyes again, she nodded. "Izzy's right about you."

Before he could ask "About what?", Izzy exploded into the room like a smiling tornado. She never just entered a room; she filled it. "Kaaaaaren teexxxxxxted," she said in her sing-song way. "They've been waaaaaiting in the car for, like, five minutes, and you know how Kimmy gets."

Paul had no idea how Kimmy got, but he followed anyway. He stood just as Anne did, and the two of them looked at each other. In need of instant awkwardness? Just add Paul. He tried to think of something, anything, to say. Still smiling a crooked smile, Anne reached out her hand. "Nice to formally meet you, Paul." He noticed her soft skin, but her handshake was firm. Very firm.

Uh-oh. Paul hadn't been ready for a firm handshake, and he hadn't situated his hand correctly, so she squeezed his limp, floppy hand. Up and down. Oh noooo . . . A total dead fish. She glanced at his hand. Disgust? Disapproval? She released it and stepped back. Paul wanted to say, "Hold on. I need a do over," but Izzy yelled "Come oooooonnnnnnn!" while bouncing to the door.

He followed obediently and turned around at the door. "Don't forget your bike," Anne said. Paul mumbled that he'd come get it later.

Already laughing as he climbed into the back seat of the car, Izzy turned to him. "I hope you brought the textbook because I totally didn't bring it home today."

"It's OK," Paul said. "I've got it."

After that day, Paul saw Anne in the hallways at times, and they'd nod, but nothing of note happened until one day about a month later when Todd Dooley and he were out in the woods behind the school. Don't get the wrong idea. Todd Dooley and Paul hanging together surely ranked as one of the all-time social hierarchy oddities in the history of Joan Pucelle High School because Todd Dooley and Paul had never hung out before—and they never did again.

Todd grew sideburns by the time he was eleven and veiny muscled arms at age fourteen. At seventeen, he talked about cars, girls, and fights. Everything else was "gay." Todd cut school randomly and received suspensions regularly. Paul had heard from two people that Todd once stood up in the middle of Geometry class, strolled right past the teacher, chucked deuces, and walked out. He said he didn't need a high school diploma because his father owned a landscaping business.

Paul thought Todd's mere acknowledgement of his existence made him cooler. Everyone in school knew Todd and had strong opinions about him. Paul, on the other hand, existed on the periphery of the cusp of invisibility. Not disliked but for the most part a ghost in the hallways, always watching and witnessing but unable to effect anything or connect with anyone.

Todd had no official role or job on the school newspaper. Never once assigned a story, instead he'd write columns about the stellar education at the school and how friendly and caring everyone was. He used effusive, over-the-top language about how fortunate the students were that perfect and precious Joan Pucelle High School even existed. Pretty much everyone understood the sarcasm, except the principal, who read a paragraph of his piece over the loudspeaker. A legendary feat. Even the people who hated Todd congratulated him. Instead of just saying thanks, Todd, crowded in a sea of sycophantic denim-and-leather-clad acolytes, rolled his eyes and murmured insults at everyone who complimented him.

At the regular Tuesday newspaper meeting in the ELA classroom, Todd could tell that the student editor, Trudy Walton, disliked his next piece. Trudy didn't come right out and refuse to run it, but while staring at her MacBook she repeatedly said out loud to nobody in particular that "There might have to be some cuts . . . I don't know" while avoiding his stare.

"You have to understand, there's just no room," she finally said to Todd, who came over the other side of the desk to look over her shoulder at her MacBook.

"Oh, but there's room for an interview with Mr. Fartsalot?" he asked.

"Look, I'm a junior," she said, avoiding Todd's menacing stare and looking to her friends for support. "I have to be here next year after you graduate."

Todd pushed himself back, took a mad step toward Trudy, and spun around. The guy had just pirouetted and yet maintained his status as the most menacing guy in the school. He was about to add something spiteful, but instead just said "I need a smoke" and stormed out.

"It's easy to be snarky," Trudy said once the sound of his clomping boots faded. "It's harder to tell the truth and . . . stuff." She looked over at Paul, and he responded with a noncommittal lift of his eyebrows, which could mean anything. Trudy took it as support.

After Paul submitted his interview with Mr. Farsala, he left for his locker. He heard Todd before he saw him. Clomp, clomp, clomp . . .

Todd wore big black work boots every day. Paul had once seen him kick a senior in the chest in the cafeteria. The kid had squared up and raised his arms like a boxer and even bounced on his feet like he'd seen on television, but Todd stood stone still, smirking, before lifting his knee to his chin and implanting his boot in the kid's sternum. Some joked that the kid's heart would forever have the word "Timberland" tattooed onto it. The kid flew back ten feet, sliding on the floor, his eyes wide and every ounce of oxygen expelled from his lungs. None of the teachers even moved. They just stared at each other until Todd clomped out.

So, when Paul heard Todd clomping his Timberlands extra hard that day after the newspaper meeting, he tensed.

"Cowards, right?" Todd yelled to the ceiling. Unsure if he was even speaking to him, Paul grunted a sound that could have been taken as amusement or agreement. He still wasn't sure if Todd was acknowledging him specifically until Todd slammed his back into the locker next to Paul's. Todd's pupils were wide and covered most of the brown in his eyes. "Wanna go smoke in the woods?" he asked.

Elated, Paul lowered his eyelids and shrugged, doing his best Todd Dooley.

Paul didn't know what Todd meant by "smoke." Cigarettes? Pot? He told himself he'd refuse, but in reality he just hoped Todd wouldn't offer. Since most of the students had already left, Paul regretted that nobody saw him hanging out with the coolest kid in school until Todd lit a blunt in sight of a classroom window. Then Paul hurried his steps.

They climbed the hill and stepped off the path that rose from the school to the field. Todd's steps were leaps. Paul thought Todd could've been a track star if he gave up smoking. Paul smiled at the image of Todd running a race clad in denim and leather. He also thought Todd could be a strong writer and probably would've been editor if calling everyone a "Nazi asswipe" or "pretentious coward" wasn't his go-to response to any disagreement, question, or compliment.

Todd collapsed in the hard brown dirt and dead weeds with his back against a tree overlooking the football field. Paul scanned for a tree to lean against, but none were close enough, so he sat with his legs crossed a few feet away facing the same general direction.

Todd stared at his joint after inhaling and then at Paul as if making a decision. Finally, he mumbled that he would've offered but he just couldn't part with "the expensive shit."

"Ah, the good stuff," Paul said attempting coolness but instantly regretting it. Todd smirked but didn't care enough to comment.

An awkward silenced ensued.

"Hey, it would be awesome if you just didn't turn in your interview and that bitch would be forced to run my column," Todd said.

Ah. Mystery solved. That was the reason for Todd's invitation. But Paul didn't care. He pretended to be pissed. "Dammit. I already submitted it, but I totally would've done that."

"Screw it," Todd muttered. "Never mind. Whatever."

The two exchanged lewd comments about the girls' lacrosse team practicing on the football field below them until Todd lectured Paul about which of the girls were "secret sluts" and which girls "wanted it." To him there weren't any other kinds of girls. Paul told him about a time he found a stash of porn mags buried in the woods behind his neighborhood. Todd smirked.

When the coach blew his whistle, Todd said he'd heard stories about the guy and called him a "closet perv."

They watched the girls scrimmage and heard Anne Prince directing her team in red pinnies. Anne received the ball on an inbound play, and a swarm of black pinnies surrounded her.

Trapped, goal line extended, Anne cradled the yellow ball on the side away from her opponents who got up on her, pushing her with their sticks and bodies. Using her own body to protect the ball from her opponents, she ran straight toward her own goal.

"No, no, no!" her coach yelled. Her teammates yelled for her to "cheap it," which meant flinging the ball up field to get it away from her net. Two girls violently bodied and stick-checked Anne, but she continued cradling the ball and running effortlessly across the field.

As she approached the end line, where she'd be forced out of bounds, she turned up at the sideline and put some distance between her and the defenders without breaking pace. Three defenders sprinted from midfield to cut her off, so Anne cut not away from them but toward them, so they all had to stop, turn, and accelerate. But they responded too late.

Now at midfield, Anne angled back toward the left, cradling the ball. She dashed toward the goal, the defenders triangulating around her and the goalie fully committed to her, leaning into the right corner. That's when Anne flicked the ball to a streaking teammate who no one else had noticed, and she tossed the ball easily into the open net.

The whistle blew, and the girls cheered. "You dirty, girl!" her teammates yelled at Anne, smiling. "You dirty!"

The coach gathered the girls for a few words and then sent them to hunt balls in the grass around the field. They marched by on their way back to the school, unaware of the boys' presence. The scraping of their cleats on the gravel created a consistent bass beat to the girls' high-pitched voices and laughter. The coaches followed, mumbling in earnest discussion.

Todd and Paul looked back to the field where Anne ran alone from one end to the other. Long toned legs, black hair, and sharp shoulders. Not jogging, running wildly, almost out of control, leaning forward so precipitously that her legs pistoned to prevent her from falling forward. Her feet sprang out behind her, and her arms jabbed the air in front of her. It was like watching a juggler, half in amazement and half for the seemingly inevitable crash.

The two squinted and raised their hands above their eyes to shield them from the setting sun, which streaked the sky in a dazzling show of orange, red, and purple. Under the freshly painted yellow goalpost, Anne dashed, stopped, checked her watch, and launched herself yet again. After two more trips up and back, she paused and dropped to one knee in the grass. The boys held their breath waiting to see if she'd relent. Slowly, she rose, raised her head, and stared at the distant goalpost. After a few seconds, she exploded forward again, and Paul let out an unintentional laugh.

They were a silent audience for forty-five minutes. The distance between them and the field might as well have been from there to the moon. Paul thought Anne was unlike anyone he'd ever met.

Anne raced back toward their side of the field, silhouetted against the sun. Her arms daggered upwards. Her first steps slammed into the earth, but within moments it appeared as if her feet hardly contacted the ground. She seemed above it. Exhausted, she paused, checked her watch, inhaled, and exploded again.

Todd and Paul didn't speak. They watched her run relentlessly as the horizon settled into vermillion. Finally, Anne lifted her water bottle, slung a bag over her shoulder, and for a moment just stared at the sky. Then she turned and walked up the hill, her cleats stamping on the asphalt path.

Just as she almost passed, Todd cleared his throat. Anne turned her head, her eyes finding Paul. From her vantage point, she could only see him. She smiled and waved her hand from side to side, her right elbow tight against her side. Paul felt the heat rise to his cheeks. He wanted to say something, but he didn't even know what. Apologize? Explain how impressive he thought she was? Ask her why? How?

But he hesitated. Todd craned his head out from behind Paul and said, "Hey, baby," sticking his tongue out lasciviously. The light in Anne's eyes disappeared, and her hand dropped to her side. She looked at Todd emotionlessly and then back at Paul, who wanted desperately to say something, to tell Todd to shut up, then get up and storm away with her. Something.

But he didn't. He stared blankly at her and then looked slightly away. He heard her cleat scrapes whisper into nothingness.

"Bitch," Todd whispered.

Paul nearly nodded in agreement but just gave his noncommittal eyebrow raise, saving himself from further disgrace.

"Do you think she'll rat us out?" Todd asked, staring down the path.

"No," Paul said. "I think she stopped thinking about us the moment her eyes turned away."

In the following days, Paul found himself bringing up her name derogatorily in front of others just to hear what they thought about her. Soon, it became assumed knowledge among his friend group that he didn't like Anne, and because of that, Izzy sometimes felt free to share little stories or complaints about her sister with him. She mostly mentioned little things, like how Anne always checked to make sure she'd done her homework and how she was "super Catholic" and wouldn't drive Izzy to the pool if certain friends were there because she didn't think they were good people.

"Which friends?" Paul asked.

Izzy said it didn't matter.

One night at a party three days after their graduation, Paul sat on the couch in front of a tray of deviled eggs under a silver-and-blue "Congrats Grads" banner on the paneled wall. The parents of whoever held the party were upstairs and only came down about once an hour, so the graduates took turns surreptitiously raiding the bar in the basement while others kept watch. Izzy, in a yellow dress that made Paul forget all the other dresses, swished by and collapsed next to him with a sigh. The smell of hard alcohol overwhelmed her perfume. She flicked her eyes toward him without turning her head.

"My sister warned me about you," she said, wagging her finger playfully, her syllables melting into one another.

"Why?" Paul laughed as if they were all grown up now, and high school concerns had long dissolved into inconsequence.

"I mean, she got it in her head that I liked you or something, and she kinda, like, cautioned me to be careful around you."

Wait, what? Record scratch. World stop revolving. "She thought you *liked* me?" he asked, attempting to moderate his tone.

She turned her head toward Paul, her green eyes alarmed as if she just overheard her own words. "I guess now that we're all going away to college, it doesn't matter anyway, right?" She stared at Paul for a moment longer, daring him to argue. But Paul was too busy internalizing this earth-shaking info and enjoying alternate timelines in his head in which Izzy walked down the school hallways hand in hand with him or everyone seeing her laugh at a joke he had told. It would've changed everything. Everything! If Izzy, the most beautiful girl in school, liked him, the entire fulcrum from which all daily high school activities rotated would have altered.

"I wish you would've said something," he mumbled, trying to maintain eye contact but failing.

She laid her head back on the sofa and closed her eyes. "Well," she announced with a hollow laugh, "too late now."

Paul walked away imagining how great his life almost was.

5

"THE MAN PROSECUTED HIS own father," Tyrese Brown told Paul over a cup of steaming coffee in the café in the basement of the Thebes county courthouse. "You asked me about Edward Prince. That's the first thing you need to know."

Paul had flown to Thebes, and his first stop was the courthouse. After a few thwarted attempts to learn more about Edward Prince, he met Tyrese Brown, who was more than willing to be interviewed.

About fourteen years earlier the tile-manufacturing company where Tyrese had worked for nearly two decades announced they were relocating to Florida. But Tyrese said he was stubborn, maybe even more stubborn than blind, and he was completely blind. "People only go to Florida to go to Disney or to die," he told Paul, "and I didn't want to do either."

So, Tyrese found a new career as one of dozens of visually-impaired Pennsylvanians operating cafes in a variety of federal, state, and local government facilities. Based on the federal Randolph-Sheppard Act, passed in 1936, which guaranteed blind people the first right of refusal on vending operations, Pennsylvania passed its own version for state and county facilities.

Tyrese didn't just make coffee and sandwiches. People told him just about everything, and he heard even more. In fact, a following had built up around Tyrese, and people came to him for advice. Some even suggested he had a gift of foresight but then laughed after they said it to show *they* didn't believe that, though maybe others did.

Tyrese told Paul that Prince's brother, Milton, a defense attorney, had been named district attorney. "I'll tell you this," Tyrese said, "it feels like a storm in the making."

Paul said he had checked his weather app and didn't think so.

"When people ask, I answer," Tyrese added. "Doesn't mean they listen, y' unnastand?"

Leaning over his counter, Tyrese, wearing dark glasses, told Paul a great deal about Edward and Milton Prince.

Edward was a true believer in justice. His obsession, however, made him difficult to control. "Lots of people tore their hair out over that man," Tyrese said. "But the harder you shook him, the tighter he clamped down."

He told Paul about the day Edward passed and that he doubted the body had made it to the morgue by the time the party chair had a replacement in mind. "You wanna listen, young man. Be sure when you do something you're doing it because it's right, not for what people might think a' you. The truth is, the moment you're gone, ninety-nine percent of people won't give you another thought."

Paul thanked him for that depressing thought and then turned their conversation toward politics. Tyrese told him that finding a replacement Senate candidate for Edward Prince would be easy because people were "crawling outta every corner for that job like demons drawn to sin." But the state constitution stipulated that "if the district attorney dies, resigns, is removed, disappears or is permanently disabled from performing the duties of his or her office, the board of county commissioners shall appoint an interim replacement."

"Now, and this is important, Frank Whipple is not just the county Republican chair but also the state party chair, y' unnastand, and he had to decide who would succeed Mr. Prince as DA. But you have to be careful who you pick. The DA can put people in jail. And the one who can jail others is the one with the real power. And the Republicans have held power in this county for so long they don't want no one from the other party snooping around.

"Now, let me tell you something. Edward Prince hired the best man for the job as assistant DA, and that man just happened to be a woman, Susan Doyle. Now you might hear a lot about her, but she got the job because she earned it. However, because of how things went down, nobody wanted her named district attorney. So, ol' Frank Whipple wanted someone who had a good chance of getting reelected. He suggested Milton Prince, and the commissioners jumped on board. After that it all took less than twenty-four hours."

Milton Prince had been a successful defense attorney. A fixture at the courthouse with many clients, sometimes he even acted as a public defender pro bono. Just about everyone respected him, even though many considered him a little . . . preachy. Milton could often be overheard telling

Edward things like, "The prison population has increased by 700 percent since 1980" or "An African American is almost four times more likely to be arrested for marijuana possession than a white person."

"The man tells anyone with ears his ideas for criminal justice reform, and my ears work fine," Tyrese said.

Not a typical first choice as a district attorney, Milton had one thing Frank Whipple thought necessary to win the race for district attorney—the name. People in Thebes County had voted for the name "Prince" for eighteen years. Most of the voters would step into the voting booth, close the curtain, see the name "Prince" on the ballot, and pull the lever.

"That's politics," Tyrese said. "But it ain't all bad. I knew a young woman who hadn't spoken to her father, a congressman y' unnastand, for ten years. You know the way young people are. Hell, it's the same way old people are. We all think we got time to fix things eventually, but eventually comes and goes. Anyway, when the congressman passed, the local party begged her to run. She scrapped her married name right quick and won. And you know what happened? She ended up staying in Congress for eight years and doing as good a job as any of them. In the end, she decided to retire from Congress and spend more time with her kids to avoid making the same mistakes her father did because she saw a lot of him in herself. I think that's a nice story."

"I'm not sure I understand the point," Paul said.

Tyrese ignored his comment and told him the police weren't exactly tossing their billy clubs in the air in celebration over having a public defender as district attorney, but Whipple assured them he'd be fine.

Paul asked Tyrese if he'd spoken to Milton about his appointment.

"Hmmmm," he said. "I like him. I do. He's a real believer in social justice. I respect him. I do. But a lot of people, when they ask you something they just want to hear what they already think said back to them, but that's not what you get when you ask Tyrese a question. I told Mr. Milton he shouldn't take the job. Now, he didn't wanna hear that. I think he felt a little betrayed, and I'm sorry for that. He said we'd spoken for hours about how to reform the county, and now it could all actually be implemented. Things like how police departments enforce the law in communities of color and reducing the population of incarcerated juveniles. 'All that's admirable,' I told him, but, 'Mr. Milton, you got me all wrong. I think you'd be good for the county, but I don't think the county would be good for you.'"

"He said he hadn't come down to spar with me and then stomped away. Before he left the café I said, 'Mr. Milton, there's blind, and then there's blind.' He said he didn't know what that meant. 'You're not your brother,' I said. Well, I could almost hear him grinding his teeth on that one all the way from here. He told me if I had something to say to just say it. So I did. I said, 'Don't take the job because you want the job so bad.' Next I heard we got ourselves a new DA."

6

PAUL CHECKED INTO A two-story brownstone hotel. After staring at the ceiling for a few hours, he abandoned his nightly attempt at sleep and rode the elevator to the lobby. The woman who'd cheerily checked him in a few hours earlier stood outside the automatic doors blowing nicotine vapor from her mouth and didn't glance up as he passed.

He had a few hours before Edward Prince's funeral, so he decided to drive around his old neighborhood. There were no other headlights on the dark roads of Thebes. His hometown hadn't changed much in the six years since he left. He hadn't stayed in touch with any friends, so he didn't call anyone. He didn't know who he'd call anyway. He actually wanted to avoid any childhood friends, so he didn't have to smile through one of those exhausting "Hey, how the hell are you, chief?" interactions that would retroactively ruin his memories of them. He thought it better if they just existed forever under the bleachers at Kennedy Park throwing snowballs at buses.

Childhood friendships were strange. When people grew up, friendship was contingent on other things like working together or living across the hall from one another. It was just accepted that the moment a person started a new job or moved, they'd establish new friendships. After some errant texts, the cord would snap and, hey, no hard feelings. But childhood friends were different. Kids believe friendship is forever, so people felt guilt or embarrassment that they didn't end up meaning all that much to one other after all.

That's how it had been with Paul's family. His parents divorced and scattered like shrapnel just weeks after he left for college, as if his departure was the starting gun for their preferred lives. His mother moved in with her divorced sister in North Carolina where they drank wine on their porch, worked part time, and drank more wine in the community hot tub.

His father remarried and started a new family in Texas. The few times they spoke, his father seemed like a different man altogether as he laughed about his brilliant and strong three-year-old son. Paul thought about it, and he couldn't remember one time when his father had laughed before. Not one. He was sure he must have, but Paul couldn't remember it.

He nearly drove by his old house but realized just before making the final turn that he had no interest. Eventually, he pulled into an empty gravel parking lot in front of St. Stephen the Martyr's Church. A rose tree stained-glass window stood prominently in the front of the church above large brown wooden doors. A buttressed tower rose above trees in the back. Paul walked alongside a low black steel gate that separated the church from a field of crooked gray gravestones, some dating back to the 1800s.

The church's bell tower had tolled three times per day for a century, but when newer upscale housing developments were built nearby in 2010, a group of residents hired a lawyer and sued over what they called "noise pollution." The pastor resisted, but the bishop announced the church would cease tolling the bells for fear of offending others in our pluralistic society. The diocese agreed to only play a recording of bells on Sundays for its noon mass.

Paul pulled at the large wooden door and was surprised when it opened. Did they leave it that way twenty-four hours a day? He'd never thought of his hometown as particularly safe, but he couldn't remember any local atrocities, repulsive acts of depravity, or even tabloid-worthy crimes.

Paul remembered one time a brown bear wandered into the Andrews' pool area and curled up under a lounge chair in the darkness until Mr. Andrews came out for a swim in the morning, screamed, and called 911. When animal control approached, the bear stomped out onto the edge of the diving board and teetered momentarily before leaping into the pool and landing on an inflatable raft.

The bear delivered a look of perfect bewilderment, having intended to jump into water but instead found itself floating as if it might just use the cup holder. The creature looked quizzically at Mr. Andrews' camera. A video of it went viral, but some animal rights group co-opted it by adding context, explaining animal control had sedated the bear and re-leased it somewhere in the Pocono Mountains, only to destroy it when it returned a week later. The postscript informed viewers that the Andrews had a low-hanging bird feeder that had attracted the bear. Made it a lot less funny, but still . . .

Paul entered the church and eased the door closed behind him. As the reporter who had broken the original news about Edward Prince's death, he hoped to go unnoticed.

As soon as he crossed the threshold, he encountered an unfamiliar quiet. Oddly, it reminded him of his first night at the newspaper. He had labored over an article about a minor zoning ordinance change. He crafted the language, gathered quotes from experts, and edited the hell out of it until all the other reporters left for the night. When he sent it to his editors, he looked around the quiet empty newsroom with its large red Pulitzer banners waving slightly in the air conditioning. Sometimes he would attempt to recapture that feeling about his work, but half the cubicles were empty now, and the Pulitzer banners seemed like graduation photos of kids long grown adorning a grandmother's wall.

Paul chose the darkest corner in the back of the church. The red-and-blue stained-glass windows portrayed images of benevolent saints and angels with swords. Shadows danced on the stone walls, created by the flickering candles lit in remembrance of whispered prayers no one would ever hear.

Metal engravings depicting Jesus' suffering, trial, and crucifixion hung on the walls with small descriptions underneath. Paul sat between Jesus's scourging and some rando lifting Jesus' cross.

How had such a faith spread all over the globe, promising misery and pain? Paul remembered enough to know Christians were supposed to emulate Jesus. Pick up their cross. Follow him. How had that request changed the lives of so many millions of people throughout history? Fewer now in this modern age but still, Christianity remained the single greatest animating force in millions of lives.

He looked up toward the large crucifix in front of the church. Perhaps in a bygone age where suffering was commonplace, Jesus' crucifixion allowed people to feel understood. Perhaps the ease of modern life made Christianity less necessary and modern comforts made Jesus less accessible. Maybe older people grew more religious simply because they'd known loss and pain, and it consoled them to know their Creator understood. On top of consolation, it offered them a happy ending, a cessation of suffering.

The church offered understanding and the promise of a better future, which, Paul noted, were the cornerstones of every successful political campaign he'd ever covered. He questioned why humans felt such an overwhelming desire to be understood and figured it must be some evolutionary urge because humans couldn't survive on their own, so only those who congregated in communities and sacrificed for each other survived the dangers of a harsh environment. Due to our need to survive, we were bred to be team players. It was in our DNA. Voila! Mystery solved. Paul congratulated himself for explaining all religions so logically.

No one had yet arrived, so he looked at the art adorning the church's back walls. It seemed different from all the other works he'd seen.

Paul's freshman-year girlfriend was an art major who made it her mission to educate the savage suburbanite in the ways of art. She dragged him to museums where he'd stare at triangles with mustaches and splatter paintings that looked like cartoon crime scenes. She'd ask how each piece made him feel, and he'd admit, "I feel nothing."

But the art in that church was different. The violence of a painting titled "The Death of Saint Peter Martyr" unsettled him. Peter's eyes focused not on the descending sword but the winged cherubs in the trees. The saint's finger inscribed words into the earth. Paul googled it and learned that the martyred saint had declared his faith even as he was killed. The angels in the trees carried the palm of martyrdom.

He couldn't help but wonder why the chubby angels didn't intervene. Paul thought if he were being killed and some stupid angels watched from a tree branch waving a leaf around, he'd be pissed. Wouldn't Christianity be more impressive if the angels saved the man? He couldn't comprehend the painting, but it was better than paint sprays or metallic junk with jutting pieces. Why had art become so removed from regular people? What piece of wisdom passed from generation to generation for centuries had been rejected? Why?

The sounds of a door opening on the far side of the church jolted him from his thoughts. An older man in a dark suit and slicked-back gray hair emerged silently from a door that looked like part of the wall pulling a massive brown polished wood coffin on wheels. Another man, also clad in black, pushed. They moved deliberately and never looked at Paul. They didn't talk about sports or their wives or check their phones.

They rolled the casket about halfway up the front aisle and then opened it to reveal Edward Prince in a dark suit with black tie. The wounds Paul had seen on his face in that hotel room were concealed. The older man reached in and adjusted Edward's jacket while the younger man busily arranged flower arrangements of lilies, chrysanthemums, and gladioli around the coffin; some on the ground, others adorning lightweight tripods.

The two men took their place at the back of the church near the doors, their hands clasped in front of them, motionless, just as Anne and Izzy entered.

Paul sank down into the pew and tried not to look at them.

7

THE PRINCE SISTERS WORE black. Anne genuflected immediately while Izzy removed her coat, revealing a tight sleeveless black dress that Paul thought looked like something she may have worn to a dance.

Her large green eyes darted warily around the church, and her shoulders slumped in mourning, but for Paul, anything conflicting with his image of her at seventeen was discarded. He watched her slender hands smooth the black coat she laid over the pew and attributed it to her manic energy.

Izzy followed her sister up the aisle toward the coffin and reached out for Anne's hand, not as a lost child would but as one offering comfort. Anne knelt at the coffin with her head down and eyes closed. Izzy stood behind her, which Paul perceived not as hopelessness but strength.

Anne rose, hugged her sister, then walked her back down the aisle toward their mother, who was being held up at the elbows by two middle-aged blond women. Izzy sat next to her mother as Anne greeted everyone who entered the church.

The assemblage soon grew so large that the outer ring pushed to where Paul was sitting. Relatives filled the main aisle nearest to the coffin. Those who'd worked for Prince gathered around the doors of the church while "Team Miscellaneous" leaned against the wall closest to Paul. A few looked his way but turned away when they didn't recognize him. He hadn't attended many funerals, but he found it odd how people gathered around a casket and discussed everything except the reason they were all there.

Paul didn't notice Susan Doyle enter the church, but all conversation ceased, replaced instantly by the urgent hiss of the wide eyed urging one another to look toward the door.

There she was. Susan Doyle wore a black coat and scarf around her neck, her blond hair pulled loosely back.

Mrs. Prince's sisters moved too late to block her vision, and she slumped as if a great weight had just been added to her slight frame.

Susan almost tiptoed as though she were traversing a minefield. The people parted in front of her and avoided her eyes. As she approached the coffin, every eye fixated on her.

"Ho-o-Oly-yy crap," said a man standing behind Paul with a man bun and circular glasses, elongating the word into five syllables. Paul turned and acknowledged him with a nod as if to say he couldn't believe it either.

Susan turned away from the coffin and searched for a friendly face. Seeing none, she made her way along the outer ring and stopped on the outskirts of Team Miscellaneous near Paul. She looked nervously at her hands clasped at her belt, at the Virgin Mary statue, and finally up at the cross. Eventually, she noticed Paul staring and smiled an uncertain polite smile. Paul half stood. "Sorry for your loss," he said before realizing how wildly inappropriate that was. Those were the exact words he'd said in the hotel lobby when he'd met her. He saw recognition in her eyes, and her face twisted away in disgust, only to see Izzy charging toward her through the crowd with Anne tugging at her from behind. Izzy stopped directly in front of Susan.

"Izzy, no. Not here. Please," Anne whispered, but Izzy's eyes quivered with . . . anger? Insult? Wrath? Susan looked down, so Izzy brought her face in close like a fighter at a promotional event. Izzy searched for words, her breath emerging in shallow, scorching gasps.

"What . . . are you . . . thinking?" Izzy hissed.

Susan stepped back. "I just came to pay my respects," she whispered.

"Respect?" Izzy jumped on the word. "Respect? You're kidding me. I can't even . . ." She looked around as if confused until her eyes settled coldly back on Susan.

"I really need to speak with you," Susan whispered, looking over Izzy's shoulder to Anne.

And then it happened. Izzy spit in Susan's face. A collective gasp. Susan snapped her head back and stepped away as Anne stepped between them.

"You seriously didn't just say 'respect,' did you?" Izzy yelled over her sister's shoulder as Anne pulled her back.

"Izzy," Anne said sharply. "This. Is. Over."

"I'm so sorry," Susan mumbled, wiping her face. Anne reached out to Susan as she passed but was too late. Susan ran outside alone.

Izzy collapsed like an imploding building and leaned her face against the back of the wooden pew inches from Paul. She wept with great heaving sobs. Anne wrapped her arms around her sister as Paul turned away and slunk deeper into the pew.

8

SOME PEOPLE ARE BORN with the ability to walk into any room and sense the mood. The portly priest who entered from behind the sanctuary did not possess that gift.

Few even noticed him. Most were still murmuring about what just happened as Father Peter Quinn ambled around offering reassuring nods and handshakes to people clearly resentful that they had to take the time to smile through small talk. Many rolled their eyes as he walked away.

Fr. Quinn approached Mrs. Prince, who stood with the help of her sisters, like a marionette. He spoke in hushed conciliatory tones, but she merely nodded as if her head weighed too much for her shoulders. Finally, her sisters mercifully explained she wasn't up to talking and lowered her into her seat.

Easy conversations inevitably turned awkward in his mouth. Fr. Quinn knew that chitchat wasn't his thing. Simple exchanges with cashiers, toll takers, and parishioners got weird when he asked too many direct questions or overshared.

Fr. Quinn introduced himself to a young woman and asked her how she knew the deceased just as a tall, regal-looking man in a black suit entered the church through the front doors. The woman looked over the priest's shoulder and excused herself. Many others passed by Father Quinn on their way to shake the man's hand. Milton Prince greeted each with a grim look and a nod, already looking on to the next person. Sometimes he took a person's hand in both of his. He never introduced the young man who followed a step behind and sometimes whispered in his ear.

"I'd go say hi to Milton, but I'm not sure if I should offer my condolences or congratulations on the new job," "Man Bun" whispered. His friend covered his laugh by turning toward the wall.

Milton never ceased moving through the crowd, receiving condolences, and shaking hands. Father Quinn, on the other hand, had settled into a long, quiet conversation with an inconsequential bespectacled man in an ill-fitting gray suit leaning against the organ.

Milton approached the priest from behind and thanked him for coming. With his left hand, he patted the priest's back. Fr. Quinn noticed the young man following Prince and stepped back to include him, but the young man looked down at his phone and remained on the periphery. The priest asked Milton how he was holding up, but he'd already moved on.

After an awkward pause, even the bespectacled man wandered away in Milton's wake.

Fr. Quinn slowly made his way to the coffin and folded his hands in prayer, which some took as a signal for silence. A white-haired organist settled onto her stool and played "Rhosymedre" as Fr. Quinn disappeared behind the sanctuary. Anne and Izzy approached their mother and escorted her to the front of the church.

Paul thought the organ music didn't so much end the silence as accompany it, focus it. He recalled how he used to study with earbuds and found some songs distracted him while others focused him. He thought it interesting that the church, an antiquated institution from a darker age, knew this.

Paul hadn't grown up religious. His parents were Baptist, at least nominally. He'd come to think of people of faith the same way he thought of soccer fans. Sometimes they met on weekends and did soccer things.

The chubby priest emerged from behind the sanctuary in a green vestment with a golden cross on the front as the undertakers wheeled the coffin to the front and closed it for the final time. With that heavy sound, Mrs. Prince let out a moan of pain that moved many in the church to tears.

Fr. Quinn opened his arms and welcomed all, his voice carrying throughout the sanctuary. He seemed . . . bigger. Swinging a single-chain thurible that emitted smoke from incense, the priest circled the coffin as the organist sustained mournful notes.

Following a series of prayers, Anne rose from the first pew, genuflected, and stood behind the podium. "A reading from the second Book of Maccabees," she said in a firm, deliberate, and careful voice. "Judas, the ruler of Israel, took up a collection among all his soldiers, amounting to two thousand silver drachmas, which he sent to Jerusalem to provide for an expiatory sacrifice. In doing this he acted in a very excellent and noble way, inasmuch as he had the resurrection of the dead in view; for if he were not expecting the fallen to rise again, it would have been useless and foolish to pray for them in death. But if he did this with a view to the splendid reward that awaits those who had gone to rest in godliness, it was a holy and pious thought. Thus he made atonement for the dead that they might be freed from this sin." She paused and then concluded. "The Word of the Lord."

In his homily, Fr. Quinn spoke about Saint Thomas More, the patron saint of lawyers and politicians, who refused to change his religious beliefs to suit the king's political needs.

"He does remember Thomas More died defending the sanctity of marriage, right?" Man Bun whispered. Paul chuckled, and several people turned around disapprovingly.

Near the end of the service, Milton delivered the eulogy and spoke about love, law, and the importance of family. Man Bun whispered that it sounded more like a campaign speech than a eulogy, earning more chuckles and angry stares.

Milton and five others carried the coffin down the center aisle and out the church doors. Edward's daughters followed solemnly. As Izzy passed Paul, she turned her head and looked directly at him. Her green eyes widened. Paul looked away.

He considered offering his condolences to her, but the thought of her looking at him with accusation in her eyes made him short of breath. He escaped out a side entrance and drove in search of a coffee shop or diner to write the most important story of his career but made a wrong turn and got lost. Could he write a story that hurt this family again? It was one thing to write about a politician, but he'd never considered the fallout. Was this even technically news? Was Edward Prince's minor national notoriety an excuse for exploiting this family?

Lost in thought, he realized he was very, very lost. He finally pulled over in an industrial park that hadn't existed when he lived there, opened his laptop, and stared at the blank screen. He didn't know where to start.

9

A CULTURAL REVOLUTION SWEPT the United States in the 1970s, tallying unprecedented victories and conquests. Since the advent of Christianity, no movement had so radically transformed an entire culture so quickly. Their success would've made Saint Peter blush.

The tectonic plates of Western society didn't just shift; they were reshuffled. The forces of secularism and the advocates of "reproductive choice" didn't just advance; they won in a rout. Within decades, progressives had a majority of judges, an entire political party doing their bidding, national media leading the cheers, and virtually all academia marching in lockstep. In short, they controlled just about all the levers of power in the republic.

Even after the legalization of abortion throughout all nine months of pregnancy, an order of nuns resisting offering insurance plans with contraception were deemed as provocations far out of the realm of acceptable behavior. Progressives insisted the cultural crisis actually worsened with each passing decade, and all their advancements existed in a state of ever-heightening peril. The 1950s perennially loomed, so what should have been a barbaric victory whoop was instead a permanent plaintive whine.

Year after year, the tasseled graduates paraded out of the halls of academia sure that the progressive secularist movement and all the rights that had been won were slipping back into the vice grips of the oppressive patriarchy.

Ensuing generations entering the halls of academia learned of the oppressive, racist, misogynistic patriarchy as a given, a truth so obvious it required no proofs. Where it was no longer visible, they called it "systemic," which meant "invisible" to anyone but those seeking it out through the prism of a PhD, like a secret decoder ring. When there were no longer parades of neo-Nazis or Klan members to hate, they settled for random white male Christians who refused to bake a cake for two men's nuptials.

It was as if progressives didn't know they had won! The word "choice" itself had become synonymous with abortion access. The leading abortion providers received hundreds of millions of dollars in taxpayer funding and performed millions of procedures each year.

And what was the pushback? What was the brutal response from the bruising grip of systemic patriarchal oppression? One random retiree standing outside a clinic gripping rosary beads in his liver-spotted hand, bellowing "God loves you and your unborn child" to women he was not legally allowed to approach.

The Elizabeth Blackwell Clinic for Women in Thebes County should have been the planted flag of the movement, the ultimate evidence of their stunning victory. The red-brick building at the corner of Main and Alcorn had once been a Catholic grammar school, closed in the 1990s and leased by Blackwell in 2012. Although the crosses and Christian accoutrement had been removed, something about the building itself was vaguely Catholic, like a former nun who still had the aura of the convent about her.

As the clinic opened on March 26, the black rubber strip affixed to the bottom of the metal door *zhwipped* across the brick outside. The growl of car engines on Main Street could be heard over the wavering voice of a bug-eyed, sign-waving, rosary-praying octogenarian, howling, "God loves youuuuuuu and your unborn chiiiiillld!" from the sidewalk.

The door closed, and the tall blond woman's sneakers chirped on the tile. She shuffled to the counter staring at her phone and mumbled, "I think I'm pregnant."

She had come in alone. They almost all did. Denice Williams' heart broke for her, not because she had accessed her constitutional right but because she'd been brainwashed to believe she should be ashamed of it.

Denice wanted to hear the woman's story, to feel her pain. To connect! For years she'd studied the significant psychological and physical injuries of the patriarchal system, enforced gender roles, and the war on women, but she yearned to stand with individual women against the selfish motives of big business, the Church, the mob, and the government.

She yearned to tell the woman in front of her that she considered her brave and empowered. Instead, as the receptionist at the Elizabeth Blackwell Women's Clinic, she simply smiled and said, "Please fill out the form, and someone will be with you momentarily."

A women's studies graduates from Bryn Mawr College, (3.9 GPA), Denice had taken the job four months earlier because she wanted to "do something," which didn't mean field phone calls, enter data, or fill out Medicaid forms, though that's exactly what filled her days. She aimed to be part of something important while working toward her PhD, and nothing was more important to Denice than overturning patriarchy, misogyny, racism, and all the systemic oppressions integral to the capitalist system.

She had friends who were app developers, lawyers, and writers for New York magazines. That was all well and good, and their mothers must have been so proud, but when she told people she was studying for her PhD in women's studies *and* working for a women's reproductive clinic, their eyes became saucers. Wow.

She imagined friends from college hearing about her life and saying things like "That's so Denice" because she'd always been the one staging anti-war rallies against American involvement in Yemen, distributing condoms in the student union, or hosting the drag queen prom. She was edgy. The tip of the spear.

On her first day at the clinic, she'd been instructed to refer to the women not as patients and never as customers. They were clients. She liked that. It felt . . . empowering. She remembered a meme she had as her home screen during sophomore year that said the word "em-pow-her" and showed a young girl screaming and punching through a wall.

On the wall behind Denice hung a pastel-blue sign with stenciled white lettering that said "Choice."

The door opened again. *Zwhip, growl.* "God loves you and your unborn child!" Another woman walked in and turned around to look at the door nervously as if the old man might come in after her.

"Don't worry about him," Denice said, waving her hand dismissively and rolling her eyes for emphasis. "He's crazy."

Denise had no idea what the man outside might have said, but he barked out there every Wednesday and Saturday. Procedure days. She'd called the police on him a few times in her first few weeks, but Allie Schine, the clinic's director, told her a police presence sometimes disturbed clients more than the cracked fool on the sidewalk.

When the professional woman returned the form on the clipboard, Denice told her someone would be with her momentarily. That "someone" was Allie, who walked clients back to the office where they spoke about insurance and payment before heading to the procedure room.

Looking over the form, Denice noticed the emergency contact hadn't been filled out. She pointed to it.

"Uh," the young woman said, "I don't have anyone."

Denice wanted to reach out and touch her and tell her she didn't need anyone, that she was enough all by herself. She yearned to celebrate her choice and tell her she should be proud of taking control of her life, but she'd been instructed to not engage.

The young woman—Susan, according to the form—didn't look up from her phone until Allie, a thin forty-something woman with black hair, a tailored pantsuit, and an office smile, approached her. Denice smelled dry cleaning product in her wake.

Eighty-seven minutes later, Denice called 911 at the behest of the heavy-set registered nurse who'd never even spoken to Denice before and whispered for her to call 911 for a client with "some excessive bleeding," low enough that the two women holding their clipboards in the waiting area couldn't hear. She also requested the ambulance park behind the clinic, so the "crazies" wouldn't see.

The EMTs pulled up behind the clinic (no siren) and rolled a gurney in the back door. They didn't acknowledge Denice as they clanked past her down the hallway. They knew the way. Denice was so worried that she couldn't sit still. She paced around her desk while listening to the muffled conversation from room five.

About ten minutes later, the EMTs rolled Susan into the hallway where Denice could see her but the two young women in the waiting room could not. Denice was relieved to see Susan awake though pale and shaking. Denice had never called an EMT before. The nurse told Susan they were just being cautious. Denice longed to say something encouraging to Susan, who stared at a brown water stain in the corner of one of the ceiling tiles.

As the red-haired EMT named Donny O'Brien discussed something with Allie farther down the hallway, Denice couldn't resist sharing some empowering thoughts with Susan. As she approached her, Susan rolled her head toward Denice. Before she could even think, Denice said, "I'll come with you to the hospital . . . if you want."

Overhearing this, Allie held up a finger to the EMT and reminded Denice of her responsibilities to the other clients. She said this as if she couldn't believe she had to.

Denice's first instinct was always rebellion. Her father called her a walking coup de' tat. She wanted to march right out of there and accompany

Susan to the hospital. She'd drink coffee in the waiting room, and when Susan felt up to it, they'd talk about rights and choice, and Denice could recommend books to read.

But the look on Allie's face told her that if she left, she would lose her job, the job that had put her in the battle and made people say, "That's so Denice." Besides, she had responsibilities at the clinic, and Susan seemed fine. She thought of all the other women she'd be unable to help if she lost her job. In the larger scheme, this instance didn't seem so important. Anyway, Susan was awake and alert. Just some excessive bleeding. They were probably just being cautious.

Susan, who for a moment looked at Denice appreciatively, lowered her head back onto the gurney and returned to staring at the ceiling. Denice looked away and hurried to the door to hold it open for the EMTs. As they wheeled her out, Susan blinked in the sun.

Denice spotted the crazy pro-lifer recording the ambulance. That would be on his YouTube channel, she thought. Yes, the old man had a YouTube channel with seven subscribers.

Denice overheard the red-haired EMT whisper to Allie that something was "unsafe" and needed to be taken care of "ASAP." Denice understood immediately. Since the nationwide trucker's strike had begun over tolls and gas prices, there had been no one to remove the biohazardous material from the clinic. In two weeks, the freezer they used to store it had overflowed. So, they stacked the blue bags inside three-gallon red buckets with the date written in marker on the top. The buckets were stacked in a small closet, and because the strike had entered its third week, a few buckets were stacked just outside the closet as well.

Each bucket displayed the "biohazardous" symbol, three circles overlapping each other like in a triple Venn diagram with the overlapping parts erased. Created by the Dow Chemical Company in the 1960s, it aimed for the symbol to be "memorable but meaningless."

Memorable but meaningless.

Allie explained to the EMT that they had a contract with a trucking company to take it away once a week, but the strike had been dragging on for over a month, and the bags had accumulated. Denice had phoned the trucking company repeatedly, but they said they were standing in solidarity with their brothers.

As the EMTs rolled Susan out the back, Denice returned to her desk. The front door opened. *Zwhip, growl,* "God loves you and your unborn chiiiiiild."

"Welcome to the Blackwell Women's Clinic," Denice said. "How can I help you?" This time she was unable to smile.

10

THE EMT REPORTED THE biohazardous situation at the Blackwell Women's Clinic, but the county health department officials, after a brief conversation over lunch that day, decided they had less than zero interest in adopting an antagonistic relationship with the only women's reproductive clinic in the county. A low-level county employee received orders to inquire about how the clinic planned to remedy the situation just in case anyone asked about the report.

Someone named K. Charleston with the title Executive Assistant to the Agency Head called the clinic and was informed they were seeking a waste vendor. Then K. Charleston filled out a form (in triplicate) that was filed in a green metal cabinet that nobody would've looked at again for years, if ever.

But the call from the county spooked Allie, who called some friends (Acquaintances? Colleagues?) she hoped she could trust in the corporate office in DC to ask what other clinics were doing about the truckers' strike. She didn't mention the call from the county for fear it would be reported up the chain. "Hope the strike ends soon," one responded sarcastically. Another suggested storing the material in a back room until the strike ended, but there was no spare room.

The threat from the county loomed in Allie's mind throughout the day. She imagined a county official with a clipboard plastering the front door with a "CLOSED" sign. She visualized the media feeding frenzy that would surely follow. She considered the disappointed call from corporate.

Then Allie decided to place a few of the dated biohazard bags in a black trash bag and toss them in the dumpster behind the building for the regular trash company to pick up. Nobody would notice a bag or two, she thought. And she was right. On Wednesday morning, upon hearing the shrill beeps of the garbage truck backing into the lot behind the clinic, she peered through the mauve curtains of her office window. Her stomach turned over, her head swam, and her pulse quickened. The big rumbling garbage truck tipped the dumpster. She tensed, waiting for something horrible to happen. Her stomach clenched, and she waited for one of the men standing beside the truck to notice something, pull out the bag, and stare at her through the curtains with an alarmed look. Or worse. She imagined one of the bags falling onto the pavement and spilling its contents in the parking lot. Disaster. Ruin.

But nothing happened. The half-asleep trash man hardly looked up, and within a minute, the truck pulled away. Gone.

Allie exhaled, pressed her hand to the wall, closed her eyes, and decided never to do that again. Too stressful. How could she have been so rash?

But every time she walked down the hall and saw the buckets piled up outside the closet, anxiety over what the county might do grew. She thought about calling the county and asking but feared that might make them act even if they hadn't been planning to do so. But if the county fined her or issued a citation, she'd never be promoted to corporate. Perhaps it would be "goodbye job." She and her husband and their twin daughters couldn't live on just his salary. She worried that if the county health department cited her, she'd be relocated to another clinic, probably in the city. The commute would be terrible. They might even have to move. But the girls were in seventh grade, and asking them to change schools would be cruel. The girls found it difficult to make friends because they always had each other, so sometimes they forgot to reach out to others. No, she couldn't do that to them.

1 1

ON THE THIRD ANNIVERSARY of his wife's death, Michael Olden stood outside the Blackwell clinic and sent his son's call to voicemail.

It had been three years to the day, so it came as no surprise when his phone rang after morning Mass as he drove to the clinic. Tim hadn't called his father in three weeks. Normally, Michael called his son at least once a week, but he'd found their conversations increasingly one sided. Michael asked how the grandkids were, about Tim's work, Tim's wife, and his summer plans. Tim's responses were either short or sounded like he might've been rolling his eyes. So, Michael didn't call the follow week or the week after that. He aimed to see how long it would take for Tim to call. Three weeks and running. So, when his phone vibrated in his pocket, Michael suspected Tim was checking a box on the anniversary of his mother's passing.

No, thank you. He rejected his son's call, sending it to voicemail.

At age eighty-one, Michael no longer had a receding hairline. Every morning he brushed back a few wisps of hair off the top of his head. Not a comb-over; it was more like he just failed to be apprised of the changing situation on top of his head. He stood outside the clinic in a blue sports coat and glasses that made his eyes appear larger than they were.

Michael walked up and down the sidewalk from 9:00—2:00 p.m. on Wednesdays and Saturdays, procedure days. He knew to keep moving, or he'd receive a citation for loitering, something he had learned from a police officer that the clinic had called on him. So, he walked to the corner of Main and Alcorn, turned around, and then returned to the edge of the clinic's property. When a car pulled in to the clinic's parking lot, he'd wait at the bottom of the walkway until they came around the side of the building. Then he'd have about eight seconds to speak to them from about fifteen yards away.

Not a poetic man or one given to hyperbole, Michael's former high school math students described him online as "so boring I wanted to jump out the window" but also a "nice old guy who always offered extra help and let us retake tests that we bombed."

Michael liked facts, and the single overriding fact of his life was that God loved everyone. Everyone. He had started "sidewalk counseling" two years before as part of a group of seven at St. Stephen the Martyr's Parish who promised to show up at the clinic on procedure days. They all did in the beginning but in just a few months, attendance became sporadic, then rare, and finally nonexistent. At the outset, Michael volunteered to pray at the clinic but didn't want to speak to women entering it. However, as the only one there, he reluctantly initiated conversation with the young women.

When he started, Michael would go so far as to offer the women a place to stay if needed. He didn't realize how creepy that sounded. Later, he attempted to explain the science of fetal development, but nobody ever stopped long enough for him to get past the word "zygote," so he thought and prayed over the one thing he could say to sum up his message and settled on, "God loves you and your unborn child." If they continued into the clinic, he would pray.

He prayed often.

He had never been the religious one. His wife, Claire, had taken the kids to Mass on Sundays while Michael slept in or did yardwork. When Claire developed brain tumors at age seventy-three, she could no longer drive because of the seizures, so he drove her to daily Mass and walked her in. It became their thing. He didn't even think of it as doing something for God. He did it for Claire. He would do anything for Claire. But somewhere along the line, he found himself paying attention, and somewhere further along the line, he believed. He couldn't point to a single moment, but his logic came down to someone as wonderful, giving, loving, and laughing as Claire didn't just happen in a random universe, so God had to exist. And Michael wanted to thank him for Claire.

In one of her final days, Claire, sitting in her chair in their living room, said maybe God allowed her to get sick, so he would start going to Mass. He responded that if God had done that to the most beautiful person in the world just so a jerk like him would believe, he didn't understand God at all. She reached out with effort and patted his hand. "Maybe he just wants us to be together forever."

"That's what I want too, honey," he said, squeezing her hand. "That's all I've ever wanted."

Three years later, on March 29, Michael prayed his rosary in front of the clinic. He used to pray on his knees, but what the doctor called "iliotibial band syndrome" made it difficult to get up and down, so he mostly stood on the sidewalk now. During the Sorrowful Mysteries, he noticed Allie Schine walking with a black garbage bag behind the clinic.

It being the twenty-first century, Michael pulled out his phone and recorded her. He always had his phone at the ready ever since a young man accompanying a girl had punched him and then tried to press charges against him.

He'd never seen Allie take garbage out before. He'd spoken to her a few times, and they once shared a pleasant conversation at the food store about a storm heading up the east coast and whether it might veer off into the ocean. In fact, he prayed for her every day.

"Mrs. Schine is taking out goodness knows what," he said aloud to his phone as if offering a play-by-play for the video. "Wait, where's she going?" he asked as she walked carefully in high heels behind the deli. Michael stepped to his left around a manicured azalea bush and held his phone up as she opened the dumpster lid, heaved a bag in, and slowly closed it. "Why on Earth is she doing that?" Michael asked. As she turned back around, he turned away but kept his phone at his hip facing her.

After Allie disappeared into the building, Michael walked around the corner from Alcorn onto Main and around the side of the deli, his phone still recording. The camera bounced, and his scuffed brown shoes moved in and out of the shot. It recorded his breath huffing and puffing, the cars passing, and his footfalls.

Michael crunched through the broken glass on the pavement behind the deli while mumbling a prayer of thanks that the back door was closed, so nobody could see him. He opened the lid of the dumpster and peered inside to see the black hefty bag. With some effort, he untied it while holding onto his phone and widened the mouth, revealing the blue biohazard bags.

"Never in my wildest nightmare," he gasped.

The phone shook as he re-cinched the bag and hurried back to his car where he stared wide-eyed into his phone. "I need to call some folks," he said.

Within eighteen hours, with the help of a fellow parishioner's youngest daughter, who had blue hair and a nose ring, a video went up on YouTube right above the video he'd asked her to put up of the ambulance taking a young woman out the back a few days before. On the video, Michael prayed, "Father, forgive them, for they know not what they do."

When he'd finished recording, he sank heavily into his favorite seat and stared at his wife's empty chair. Even though he thought it might be too late, he called his son. "Hi Tim," he said. "How are the kids?"

Comments on the YouTube video:

1. That is horrifying! May God forgive us.

2. Sicko! I don't believe anything you say. This video is clearly doctored!

3. If we don't value humanity in all its forms, we will pay a terrible price.

12

MILTON PRINCE ASSUMED OFFICE the day before his brother's funeral.

All appointees, however, were forced to face a special election within six months. When Milton asked about campaigning, Whipple told him to do absolutely nothing. If he raised his visibility, people might realize he wasn't his brother. Whipple said sending a rookie politician out to the press was like teaching a child to ride a bicycle and pushing him or her off on a unicycle over a fatal drop teeming with lions.

So, Milton merely approved quotes for press releases written by a young man who rarely looked up from his phone. Milton couldn't remember the young man's name (Alan? Walter?) but felt it was too late to ask. "Hey, I know you've been my constant companion for days, but what the heck is your name?" That would not be very "man of the people."

Alan/Walter even revised and edited Edward's eulogy for his brother with flourishes such as, "It is love that shapes us into the people we are, and nowhere is that love more apparent than in our families" and "The two animating focuses of my brother's life were family and the law. Edward acted as an advocate of the law. He pursued justice. And that has become the focus of my own life as well."

Milton certainly looked the part. At forty-five years of age, he had retained his youthful fitness due to his daily workouts with a personal trainer and a daily bike ride. In fact, Milton rode his bike to work on his first day in order to set an example for others. A strong chin. Good hair. Some graying at the temples; just the right amount. He also had all the right beliefs to fit in with the suburban Pennsylvania county, which had been a reliably red county until about 2004 when the number of Democrats moving out of Philadelphia reached a tipping point and turned the county purple, if not pink.

The party saw Milton's appointment as maintaining the status quo. And the status quo was victory.

Comments at the Philadelphia Bulletin:

1. So, this guy died in scandal. He prosecuted his own father. What god did this family piss off? They seem cursed! Hey, I have an idea, let's put his brother in charge. What could possibly go wrong?
2. This is the kind of thing that makes people roll their eyes and stay away from politics.
3. Politics at its worst. This county deserves what it gets. When the spirit of the law is broken like this, this county will fall. Anarchy, baby! Bad things will come of this.
4. We are not our family. Give the guy a chance.

13

THE VIDEO MICHAEL TOOK of Allie dumping buckets of fetal remains might have been ignored. By the end of the second day, it garnered only eighty-three views. If someone from the corporate office of the Elizabeth Blackwell Women's Clinic had seen it, they could've contacted YouTube and had it removed as offensive and/or doctored material. That would've ended it.

But a blogger at a pro-life website with about 900 views per day reposted it. A reporter for a Christian news site that received about 10,000 views per day reposted the video along with the video of Susan being taken away via ambulance from the same clinic and titled it "Is this the worst abortion clinic in America?" Deep in the article, Susan Doyle was named as the woman who'd suffered a perforated bowel, but the reporter didn't connect the name to the news of Edward Prince's death.

Nobody did. But on day three, the video had 13,000 views, one of whom was Anne Prince.

14

Izzy lay under her comforter in her bed paying little attention to the music from her wireless earbuds or the slow whirling ceiling fan blades her eyes lazily followed. Her pink heart-shaped pillow leaned back against a white wooden headboard. She didn't hear Anne's voice and hardly looked up when her bedroom swung open.

Izzy worked hard not to acknowledge Anne standing there in her red coat and blue jeans. Her cheeks were red as if she'd been running.

"Izzy," Anne said, her intense eyes glancing around the room taking in the tiny twinkling bulbs twined through sheer drapes that hung from the ceiling to the foot of her bed. At age thirteen, Izzy said it gave the room an "ethereal" look, a word she'd learned from a young adult fantasy novel. But at age twenty-three, she gave the lights no more thought than the big clunky sanded-down wooden letters above her vanity that spelled "LOVE."

As Anne glanced around the room, Izzy became aware of the mess, including her clothes from the past two days on the floor and a bowl on her nightstand. She immediately felt defensive even though Anne had simply looked around to make sure Izzy had eaten.

"Izzy, have you read or heard anything today?" Anne asked.

"No," Izzy replied with an eyeroll and pulled out just one earbud as if to say she expected the conversation to be short. "I've had my eyes stapled shut and my ears glued. You're the first person I'm seeing or hearing today."

"It's about Susan Doyle, alright?" Anne asked.

Insert eyeroll here. It had become Izzy's go-to reaction to any development in the world she didn't want to deal with, meaning pretty much all of them.

Unsure of what that particular look of disgust meant, Anne continued. "Dad's—"

"Stop it!" Izzy hissed, sitting up. What the hell? Was Anne really going to say the words out loud? "Anne, why do you have to put everything right in our face and . . . just . . . grind?"

"I'm sorry," Anne said, then took a breath. "Susan Doyle went into the hospital the day after the funeral."

"Why?" Izzy asked, pulling out her other earbud and wrapping it around her finger, an expression of concern on her face. She sat up, revealing a long blue T-shirt with a cartoon character talking to a goldfish in a bowl.

"She had an abortion, and something went wrong," Anne said.

"Good," Izzy said, leaning back into her headboard. "I hope she—"

"Please don't say that," Anne said, swiping her hand dismissively as if she knew Izzy didn't mean it. Anne stood there looking at her sister, who looked at everything except Anne. "I called the hospital, but Susan wouldn't talk to me. I think she's going to be in there for a while though. But anyway, Izzy, you're not understanding. I don't know how to say this without you getting mad at me."

"Ugh, you're really going to try to be subtle for the first time in your life?" Izzy asked.

"OK, Iz, the woman Dad had an affair with just had an abortion," Anne said, the words spilling out as if they would be easier to bear if heard quickly.

Instantly pale, Izzy slouched and leaned back on the headboard. She pulled her comforter toward her chin. "What are you saying?" she asked, still looking down.

"I don't know what you're not getting," Anne said, coming around the side of her sister's bed and sitting on the edge.

"You're saying . . ." Izzy didn't complete her thought. She couldn't.

"I'm not saying anything yet."

The word "yet" bothered Izzy. She knew how exacting Anne could be with her language. "So, is there more?"

"The way I see it, on top of losing our father, we just lost a baby brother or sister as well." She said it as if she were putting the finishing touches on a complicated word problem.

"Oh, Anne, no, no, no, you can't say it like that," Izzy ordered, her eyes wide, sitting up straight and kicking back with her legs, so her back slammed against the headboard, allowing for the greatest distance between them. "Don't even say that."

"What?" Anne countered. "The truth?"

"Isn't it already bad enough?" Izzy said. "Do you have to make it worse by saying it?"

Anne didn't answer. Izzy turned away from her sister and looked at the white wicker chair her parents had bought for her sweet sixteen party. That night it had felt like a throne. Now it sat in the corner of the room filled with old stuffed animals.

Suddenly alarmed, Izzy looked past Anne to the hallway. "You didn't say any of this to Mom, did you?"

"No, of course not," Anne responded in her "Do you think I'm an idiot?" tone. Their mother had hardly gotten out of bed since the funeral.

Izzy refused to make eye contact with her, continuing to look everywhere but at Anne.

"I wouldn't have even told you," Anne continued, "except . . ."

"Except what?" Izzy said, certain things were about to get worse.

"I read the other day that behind that clinic they've been dumping aborted fetuses in the dumpsters."

Izzy crinkled her face in disgust. "That's sick."

"There's a video, Izzy. Think about this. Our brother or sister . . ."

"Don't call it that."

". . . might at this moment be getting tossed into a dumpster for the birds and rats to feast on."

"Ugh, what's wrong with you?" Izzy exclaimed with a look of horror. "Seriously, what the hell is wrong with you, Anne?"

"Me?"

Izzy stared at her sister, then looked back toward her stuffed animals. Then something occurred to her. "Anne, why are you wearing your coat? Where are you going?"

Anne adjusted herself on the bed, moving closer to Izzy. "Come with me," she said.

"Wheeeeeeere?" Izzy demanded.

"I plan to honor our dead."

"What? Who? Where?" Izzy leapt to her knees. "Anne . . . please explain exactly—"

"I intend to take the remains of our brother or sister from there and have a funeral Mass. They're not garbage to be tossed aside."

"And you think they're just going to let you take it out?" Izzy asked, staring at Anne as if she were crazy.

"I would assume not," Anne replied, maintaining eye contact.

"That's illegal!" Izzy cried, her hands at her face. "You'll be arrested."

"There's no law against honoring the dead," Anne implored.

"But there are several laws against breaking and entering!" Izzy said. "And stealing!"

"Iz, Come with me."

"You can't be serious, Anne. Please don't do this." Izzy leaned across the bed and grabbed her sister's hand. "Our father just died. His . . . failings just made national news, and he left behind a wreck of a grieving family. Our mother can't even get out of bed. Please, please, please don't make this worse. Let's go about the business of grieving and consoling each other like normal people rather than making a crazy stand on some principle."

Anne stood. "I won't ask you to join me again. If I'm arrested, so be it . If I must break the law to serve a higher law, I will."

"Can't you just let one battle pass by?" Izzy asked. "God, you're so much like Daddy sometimes."

"Don't compare me to him," Anne said, her mouth pursed and her eyes shooting a warning.

"Sorry, sorry, sorry," Izzy said as if she hoped the mere weight of her words would change her sister's mind. "Anne, seriously, must every injustice be remedied? By you? Look, you're serious about your faith. I get it. Isn't love the highest calling though? If you do this, you'll be torturing us. Is torturing your family what God wants? Anne, honestly, this will break us. If you do this, who does it help? Nobody. Can't you think of others please please please?"

"I am thinking of others," Anne said with finality, lowering her eyes. "I've got to go.."

"Anne, no," Izzy held her sister's hand, afraid to release it. "Don't do this. Have mercy! Something awful will happen. Please don't do this. It's not our business."

"Don't be afraid" Anne said, tapping Izzy's hand.

"Anne, please listen. You're saying you're honoring the family dead, but really you're destroying your family. Is that what you want? Is it?"

"Iz," Anne replied, "our brother or sister could be tossed into a dumpster. And you want me to turn my back? You say family is important but then ask me to abandon my sibling to a dumpster?"

"So, you're, like, obsessed with doing right by the dead but damn the living, right?" Izzy said, her eyes aflame.

Anne stood. "Our father abandoned this family. I won't."

Izzy gripped her sister's fingers tighter. "Anne, don't go. Please don't do this. Please, Anne please." Anne remained silent. Finally, Izzy released her.

Before walking out of the room, Anne told Izzy that she'd made a list of medications their mother needed and detailed when she needed to eat and what. "You have to step up, Iz, OK?"

When she didn't receive a response, Anne placed the list on Izzy's bureau and then walked out. Izzy stared at the door, pulled the comforter back around her, pushed her earbuds in, and watched the fan blades revolve slowly.

Then she stood with her comforter still wrapped around her, shuffled past the bureau, went down the hall to her mother's room, and climbed into bed beside her. She wrapped her arm around her mother, and they both lay there, their eyes wide open.

15

DENICE SAW A SHADOW pass by the waiting room window. Alarmed, she looked up from her computer toward the window just in time to see a woman in a red coat pass by.

Feigning unconcern so as to not alarm the two women in the waiting room, Denice ambled over and pushed her face against the window, looking to the rear of the building where the woman in the red coat had disappeared. She couldn't see her.

"I'll be right back," Denice announced to the women, who didn't look up. She hesitated before entering Allie's empty office and then jogged to the far window, where she saw the woman in the red coat in the back of the parking lot. Denice's breath fogged up the glass, so she wiped it with her fist. The young brunette in the red coat was standing behind the clinic building. A jolt of fear surged through Denice. The old man in the front and this crazy lady in the back? She feared violence.

No, Denice told herself. It could just be a confused woman second guessing her appointment. The cracked old guy had probably said something to upset her. Yes, Denice decided that might be the case. She had to help the poor girl. She strode out of her office, down the hallway, and opened the back door to the clinic.

The girl with the red coat standing next to the dumpster turned toward her, alarmed, her eyes wide. Her coat had black smudges.

"Hi, are you OK?" Denice asked.

The girl looked around. "I'm OK. Um, how are you?"

Denice was taking in as much information as possible. Young woman, twenty-fiveish, holding a black garbage bag in her right hand. She wasn't homeless. Her nails were done with a dark-purple polish. Her shoes were expensive, her eyes clear and focused.

"Do you want to come in?" Denice asked.

"OK . . ." the girl said.

But why the bag? And why the smudges on an expensive coat? As she followed the girl up the ramp, Denice considered that she knew absolutely nothing about her and definitely didn't want her near the other clients, so she directed her to the first door on the right.

"So, you saw me out there?" the frazzled girl asked on her way in the back door.

"Yeah. Did the old man say something to you? If he did, I could call the police."

"What? No. He just told me God loves me."

"Oh." Denice had no other response.

Denice grew uneasy but wanted to help this young woman and put all her years of study to good use. "I'm here to help you. You understand that, right?" Denice said loudly and slowly.

"I believe you think you're helping," Anne said, no longer focusing on Denice but on the closet behind her.

Denice turned and saw the stacked buckets of biohazardous waste. "Oh, don't worry about those. That's nothing."

"Oh my God," Anne said, looking weak. "All those bags and buckets." She leaned her hand on the procedure table.

"We're here to help you," Denice said. "I know this seems like a big moment in your life, but this is only as important as you decide it is. Your responsibility is only to yourself."

"This place . . ." Anne said, looking around the room. "This place."

"This is a place of empowerment and support," Denice said, holding out her hands in a calming manner and stepping forward.

Anne leveled her glare at Denice and approached her. Denice backed away, her eyes wide with escalating fear.

Anne passed her and approached the buckets, then went down on one knee. She tilted her head to read the writing on top of the buckets. "It's not the right date," she said, pointing to the bucket and moving on to the next one.

"Um . . . you're not supposed to be . . . that's just soiled linens and equipment and . . . can I help you?"

Anne lifted one bucket and then another.

"Oh no . . ." Denice said and then ran down the hall to her desk.

Dispatch: 911. What's your emergency?

Denice Williams: Um, there's a strange woman in our clinic. She just walked past me and went down the hall. I asked her to stop, and she just—

Dispatch: What's the address?

DW: What? Oh, 274 Alcorn Street, Eagleville, PA.

Dispatch: OK, what's going on?

DW: A girl just walked in here, and I asked her if I could help her, but she just walked past me . . . uh . . . she just walked into another room across the hall. I don't know what she's . . . (garbled) looking for.

Dispatch: There's an unwanted person in your residence?

DW: Um, clinic. This is the Elizabeth Blackwell Women's, um, Women's Clinic, but yes there's an unwanted person here. Can you send someone? I don't know if she's just confused or . . .

Dispatch: The police have been notified and are on their way. What's your name?

DW: Denice Williams.

Dispatch: OK, Denice, stay on the phone with me. What is the person doing now?

DW: I . . . I don't know. She just walked around one of our procedure rooms. Do you want me to go check?

Dispatch: No. Stay where—

DW: Oh, she's back. She's walking toward me . . .

Another voice: Excuse me.

Dispatch: Denice? Denice? Are you—

DW: She's leaving. She just walked out. I'm heading to the door to lock it . . . It's locked. I don't see her.

Dispatch: Police will be there shortly.

DW: OK. Thank you.

Dispatch: Just stay on the line until the police arrive . . .

Twelve minutes later, at 10:40 a.m. on Saturday., March 30, 2019, Officers Shawn Hardaway and Michael Dougherty responded to a call of an "unwanted person" at the Elizabeth Blackwell Women's Clinic. They'd been called to the clinic five times over the previous three months. Each time they arrived to find a solitary old man standing on the lawn telling people God loved them. One time he'd offered to get the officers coffee from the deli around the corner.

It hadn't been difficult for police to get a description of a suspect. Denice Williams described the suspect as a Caucasian female, early twenties, black hair pulled back in a ponytail, blue eyes, five foot eight inches wearing a red coat, jeans, and blue Skechers. Denice said the woman walked out carrying a blue bag that likely contained "products of conception."

When interviewed by police, Michael Olden told them he knew the young woman who'd walked (not run) past him. "A lovely young girl," he said. "Sweet. I see her at Mass often."

When asked what color her eyes were, he said he had no idea. When asked about her height he said anywhere between five foot four to five foot nine. He didn't notice a blue bag, but he did remember a red coat. He said he'd been surprised to see her go into the clinic because he'd often seen her at Mass, but he told the officer he didn't judge people on their weakest moment. According to Michael, as the girl in the red coat passed him, she said, "God bless you for what you do here."

16

ALLIE WAS RUNNING LATE that morning. Her girls both had science projects due for a regional science fair being held at their school and hadn't worked on them until the night before, so she'd run out to a craft store for supplies, including Styrofoam balls of varying sizes, paint, and wires to create two solar systems. She found everything else in the junk drawer.

Worse yet, they were group projects, so she had to find out what the other students in the group were doing and what she had to do. So, while she built the sun, the moon, and the stars, her daughters texted their classmates.

"Girls," she said, "if you're going to do group projects, at least be in the same group because I'd rather just create one project."

Ashley and Heather said their teacher never allowed them to be in the same group because the school encouraged socialization. Allie recalled she had requested that in the beginning of the year. So, yeah, she had brought this on herself.

In the morning, the girls raced to the van for the front seat while holding their projects. Allie, following behind, scolded them, saying they could've tripped and fallen and hurt themselves and/or destroyed the projects. She lectured them the way parents lectured weakly after everything had already turned out alright.

On the way to school, Allie and the girls talked about their friends, their field hockey team, and their "totally weird" history teacher. They played their favorite song on her phone, and the two danced in their seats and recited the lyrics, which sounded to Allie like "Bum diddy bum back up your bum diddy bum bum." Allie silently questioned whether the song was appropriate for young girls but decided she didn't know for sure what the song even meant, so she said nothing.

Allie shook her head in mock disapproval but couldn't help but smile at her kids' enjoyment. A rush of gratitude overcame her for her two daughters, so overwhelming she didn't know where to put it all. She laughed out loud at their dancing, causing her daughters to sing louder and dance crazier.

She and Kyle had struggled for so long to have children. Only after three in-vitro-fertilization procedures was she able to conceive. Now her life overflowed with contentment, joy, trials, and disappointments, and she embraced it all.

She pulled onto the tree-lined campus of Hamilton Academy, past the buildings with state-of-the-art computer labs, the sprawling athletic fields, and the grand performing arts center. The two girls in their royal-blue skirts and sweaters kissed her before racing to the metal front doors of the white building, holding their fragile projects in front of them.

Allie watched to ensure they got inside. Only after the doors closed did she turn off the song and pull away. As she always did, she considered the fragility of everything and worried about losing it all. She built consequence trees and ran imaginative simulations in her mind as to how to avoid them. She had just about convinced herself that everything could be handled right up until the moment she saw two police cars parked in front of the clinic.

17

MICHAEL WAS STANDING OUTSIDE the clinic speaking with a police officer. As Allie drove up, he waved to her. Yup, he actually waved like they were coworkers or neighbors. And she shocked herself when she waved back.

Allie parked in the back lot and entered the clinic through the rear door. Denice spun around at her desk, wide eyed. "Awomancamein-andtooksomebagsofbiohazardouswastefromthebackroom . . . (breath) andicalledthepolicebutshewalkedrightpastmeanditriedtostopherbut—"

"Denice," Allie said, raising her hands. "Slow. Down."

When Allie understood a woman had entered the clinic and stole a bag of biohazardous waste, she asked Denice why she had let a strange woman in the back door.

"That's not exactly how it happened," Denice replied. "I, um, saw her outside and went to ask her, like, what are you doing? And she kind of, like, y' know, marched right in past me. I didn't invite her if that's what you mean."

"And she was looking for a specific bag?"

"Yeah. She said something about one of them not being the right date."

Officer Dougherty, a tall, beefy, sunglass-wearing, crew-cutted cop, had questioned Denice. She felt strange not telling the complete truth to the police, but Allie was right next to her. Dougherty had a way of leaning over her after each question that unnerved Denice. She convinced herself the truth would only hurt the clinic—and her. In fact, the truth wouldn't help anyone. Officer Shawn Hardaway, a short, stout African American police officer, hardly looked up from his pad as he wrote down everything she said. That unsettled her even more.

As soon as the police left, Allie called her friends in corporate for advice. Her friend, Rachel, laughed. "You called a few days ago saying you had too many buckets, and now some rando anti-abortion nut is taking them off your hands? Sounds like an answer to prayer."

Allie asked if Rachel thought she should say something about this to the media. "Absolutely!" Rachel replied. "These people pretend like they're all just praying and all that nicey-nice godly people crap. It's because we don't publicize all the evil shit they're up to."

Rachel directed press relations for the clinics in Philadelphia, New Jersey, and Delaware. She often talked about retiring with her partner to California and told Allie she'd recommend her for the job. So, in the end, Allie thought this wasn't so much a problem as an audition for the job. Yes!

18

BACK IN THEIR PATROL car, Michael Dougherty called the chief on his cell phone, something he did when a sensitive issue arose, and he didn't want the press or anyone with a police scanner app to hear. As he waited for the chief to pick up, Dougherty looked over his sunglasses at Hardaway. "A shit storm, pal. I predict a total shit storm."

The chief ordered them to find the young woman and pick her up quietly. "I don't want headlines," he said. "Don't make this a thing." Those were his orders, not to make this "a thing."

The two drove around the surrounding neighborhood in widening concentric circles for about ten minutes. They didn't believe for one moment they'd find the young woman, but at a stop sign about three quarters of a mile from the clinic, they were shocked to see a young black-haired girl in a red coat walk right in front of their car talking on her phone while carrying a blue biohazard bag in her right hand as if she didn't have a care in the world.

"No effing way," Hardaway said, smirking.

"Well, she's not exactly hiding," Dougherty observed.

The two looked at each other and laughed as she passed right in front of them. They turned the corner behind her. She didn't run. She walked.

"Where do you think she's going?" Hardaway asked.

Dougherty shrugged. "Give her a minute. The farther she gets away from the main road the better, right? We don't want this to become 'a thing,' remember?"

"Yup," Hardaway agreed.

"We'll pick her up after she passes the church up here," Dougherty said.

Hardaway nodded, and they followed in their patrol car about twenty feet behind. They watched as she passed the cemetery. They would've arrested her right there, but a group of moms with at least four children were watching them from a small park across the street. They'd wait until the girl in the red coat was out of sight of the women to apprehend her.

"She knows we're here, right?" Hardaway asked, watching the young woman walk seemingly carefree.

Dougherty nodded, not looking away from her. "She knows."

When the suspect turned right at the walkway of Saint Stephen the Martyr's Church, both officers looked at each other. "What the . . ." Hardaway's eyes widened. "Oh no. Stop the vehicle. Stop. Stop," he said and opened his passenger door with the car still rolling.

Dougherty slammed on the brakes and his partner leapt out of the car.

"Ma'am? Ma'am?" Hardaway yelled, jogging up behind her.

The young woman opened the door of the church, stepped inside, turned to face the two officers and said one simple word: "Sanctuary."

"What?" Dougherty said. "Ma'am, you have to come with us."

"Officers," she replied, "I understand you're doing your job, and eventually I'm sure I will go with you, but I have something to do right now, and I don't believe you want to enter a church when I've already declared sanctuary."

"Ma'am," Officer Hardaway said, stepping toward the door.

Fr. Quinn had already been in the church that morning for the most unspiritual but necessary reason: the HVAC system was failing. With a majority of Mass attendees aged seventy years and older, too hot and too cold were not idle concerns. Just as he was about to give up on the HVAC guy, his secretary, Judith, called to tell him a parishioner—she didn't get the name—was on her way to the church and needed to meet him urgently. Fr. Quinn asked about Judith's cat and was told about all the medical problems Pepper had suffered. He promised to keep the feline in his prayers. He hung up just as Anne walked in the door with two police officers behind her.

"Can I help you?" the short, balding priest with a ready smile asked the officers. Dougherty glanced around to see one of the moms across the street holding up her phone, recording. Crap.

"Hello, sir, um, reverend. This young woman is being detained due to a serious matter," Dougherty said. "She needs to come with us."

Fr. Quinn slipped in front of Anne. He'd known her for years. He'd arrived at the parish at about the same time that she had returned home from college. She attended Mass on Sundays and sometimes during the week even though she rarely spoke to him.

Officer Hardaway stepped toward the chubby priest. "Pastor, this young woman is a suspect in a crime. We need to speak with her now." His voice was deep. Threatening?

"Officers, I'm sure you wouldn't mind if I had a word with her first, would you?" Fr. Quinn asked. "I respect your authority, and I'm grateful for your service, but this young woman buried her father here just a few days ago and has come seeking spiritual guidance. She will not go anywhere else, I assure you.

"I should also remind you that two months ago, the bishop and the town council held a press conference in which the bishop declared all the churches in the diocese a sanctuary for undocumented immigrants, and the town council said they would honor that. The council seems to take this declaration seriously, so you may want to call them."

The two officers hesitated, and Fr. Quinn seized the moment. "You're always welcome in this church, but I ask that you allow me some time to speak with a member of my flock who is seeking guidance."

Dougherty gripped Hardaway's arm and squeezed. It was not a suggestion but an order. Stand down. Fr. Quinn didn't slam the door in their faces, as was later reported. Neither did he bar the door. He simply allowed it to close, and the officers stood there and watched it happen.

As the door shut, the only thing Dougherty and Hardaway were certain of was that this had become a thing, a very big thing.

Dougherty took out his cellphone and called the chief. "A shit storm. A total shit storm."

19

IT TOOK ABOUT AN hour for Allie to write a press release. She was proud of it. She emailed it to Denice, instructing her to send it to all the local newspapers, radio stations, and television networks.

Women seeking reproductive health care should be able to do so free from violence, intimidation, and harassment!

However, today an anti-abortion activist violated a buffer zone ordinance that keeps abortion opponents at least twenty feet from the doors or driveways of any reproductive healthcare facility and entered the Elizabeth Blackwell Women's Clinic for Reproductive Health, intimidating and frightening clients and employees and stealing several bags of biohazardous waste.

Since Roe v. Wade and the legalization of abortion, anti-choice extremists have attempted to prevent women from accessing care by any means possible. We've witnessed how some anti-women legislators have done the bidding of the far right, employing a range of radical legal and legislative tactics. On top of this, and much more horrifying, are the intimidating extra-legal tactics and sometimes violent means anti-choice zealots choose.

Since the passing of Roe v. Wade, clinics, providers, and patients have been targets of murder, bombings, arson, death threats, kidnappings, assault, harassment, stalking, and vandalism.

This violence is intended to hinder access to abortion services and threaten the lives of those dedicated to providing reproductive health care. Nobody seeking health care should have to fear for their safety or walk a gauntlet of intimidation and harassment. This is a dark day for Pennsylvania and those who work to ensure reproductive health care access to every woman.

The Blackwell Clinic is working with local authorities to bring the suspect to justice.

Smiling proudly, Allie had just finished re-reading the release when Denice knocked on her door. "Allie, the police are on the phone," she said. "They want to speak to you."

"Which line?"

"Um, the blinking one," Denice replied, then disappeared back down the hallway. Allie couldn't decide if Denice had just given her attitude or not. She lifted the phone.

"Mrs. Schine?"

"Yes."

"This is Detective Bright with the Thebes County Police. I'm calling in reference to the theft and unwanted person in your clinic earlier today."

"Have you caught her yet?"

"We're working on it ma'am."

That was definitely attitude, Allie thought. "What can I do for you officer?" she asked, intentionally saying "officer" instead of "detective."

"We have footage from your security camera, and it appears the young woman who entered your clinic also went behind the facility and removed some things from your dumpster. Do you know why this person might be interested in your dumpster?"

Allie couldn't breathe. Her mind built a consequence tree and considered calamity after calamity that could follow. If the police discovered what she had thrown in the dumpster and, oh no! the media! She'd just sent out a press release! She'd actually invited this scrutiny!

"No, I don't. I have no idea. How would . . . I'm not sure I understand . . ." she heard the words spilling out of her mouth. "Whose dumpster?" she mumbled. "No, I don't know why anyone would be interested in a dumpster."

Detective Bright thanked her and hung up. Allie sprang from her seat and ran out into the hallway. "Denice? Denice?" she called, trying to sound calm. "Did you send out the press release yet?"

Denice spun around in her chair, smiling with her hands over her heart. "Yes I did. So great. Like, profound."

Oh.

Allie wouldn't show panic. She closed her eyes and inhaled. "Um, Denice, did you see that person who entered the clinic earlier around our dumpster?"

"Actually, yeah. I told you I saw her in back, remember? Right next to the dumpster. In fact . . ." Denice walked down the hallway toward Allie as if she were trying to remember something. "Yeah, she was carrying that bag. I don't know if she intended to throw something out or . . ."

Allie walked back into Procedure Room Five and pointed out the bag still sitting right next to the table. Denice said, "I forgot about it in all the excitement. Should we tell the police? Oh my holy hell, do you think it's a bomb?"

"Go back to your desk," Allie said. "Please."

Allie stared at the bag. *Oh no.* She untied it, pulled out the bucket, and placed it with the others outside the closet. She crumpled the bag and threw it into a trashcan. Then she walked back into her office, leaned against the white wall, and concentrated on breathing while her mind considered every terrible possibility. She searched for a way out, an angle.

The bag. The girl. The video! She sat at her computer and erased the security footage of her walking out with those bags earlier in the week. She couldn't believe she hadn't thought to do that earlier. What else hadn't she thought about? The question made her sick.

Comments from the *Thebes Weekly News* website:

1. First comment!

2. What the hell do anti-abortionists want with biological remains?

3. This could be the act of a post-abortive woman. Prayers are needed, not condemnation.

4. Could be Satanists!

5. I just know they're planning some PR event with this. Disgusting.

6. What about personal choice do you not understand?

20

FRANK WHIPPLE HEARD ON the radio that an anti-abortionist had stolen biohazardous waste from a women's health clinic. The jubilant fat man contacted Milton Prince. "A perfect opportunity, a layup," he said. "I want a full press conference. I want you to be the man."

Excited, Milton asked if he should bring the police in on the press conference to show a united front. Whipple laughed. "I'll leave that to you. But Milton, the police don't like you much. You're a public defender who grilled police officers on the stand for a living. Second, the cameras love uniforms. You'll be second fiddle. Do yourself a favor, and stand in front of the microphones and promise that the guilty party will be pursued, apprehended, and prosecuted to the fullest extent of the law. Just call the chief, and make sure nobody's been arrested yet."

"You think this case is important enough for a press conference?" Milton asked, a little unsure.

"That's the question of a political infant. I forget sometimes you're still practically covered in placenta juice. Wake up, Milton. The media lives for this kind of crap. You'll get some print, probably some radio, and maybe even local television. And I love what this says about you. You're a Republican who shit-cans anti-abortion extremists. This makes you the perfect moderate for this county. You play this right, this guarantees your reelection, you lucky bastard."

"And if I win, we'll talk about implementing some of the reforms I have planned?" Milton asked.

"My friend, *when* you win, we can implement all of them." Whipple laughed and then hung up. No goodbye. Nothing.

Milton couldn't sit at his desk. His first press conference! Pacing, he texted the chief of police to see if any arrests had been made. Within a few seconds, he received a one-word response: "No."

Walter/Alan wrote and issued a media advisory announcing a press conference scheduled for 8:00 a.m. the following day.

2 1

Two DAYS BEFORE ANNE walked into the Blackwell Clinic, every cable news channel broke into their regular programs with "breaking news" chyrons about an avalanche at a family ski resort in rural Pennsylvania. That evening the network news led with the story with reporters "on the scene." With every American a potential Zapruder, the media announced "shocking new footage" from cell phones that they had downloaded from YouTube. News reporters "on the scene" interviewed witnesses who seemed shaken, horrified, or bizarrely delighted to be on television.

Moments after the overhanging ledge of snow on the ridge of Killybegs Mountain collapsed over the double-black-diamond slope, the media reported thirty-six people missing. After two hours, all but seven were accounted for. Seven were assumed dead, including a former professional hockey player who dated a sitcom celebrity.

Interviews with former teammates and avalanche experts took up much of the initial coverage, but three hours after the horrible event, rescuers pulled a young woman from a twenty-seven-foot-deep snowbank. After doctors cleared her, the mother of two with red cheeks told reporters she'd never even seen the snow coming and regained consciousness only to find herself trapped in a cave of packed ice. Her ears rang so loudly she'd attempted digging toward the sound until she noticed her breath floating toward her feet and turned herself around. She admitted she might've given up right there, but the thought of her children pushed her. So, she said a silent prayer and lunged upward time and again, her fingers stinging with cold but working desperately to loosen the packed snow around her. As she approached the surface, exhausted, a rescuer heard her burrowing and pulled her out.

One network interviewed her along with her rescuer. She cried, and he cried, and they hugged while the interviewer looked meaningfully into the camera.

For one day, Americans watching television heard experts describe that avalanches start because while most snowflakes are hexagonal and interconnect with one another, others come in odd shapes, some needle shaped. These do not interlock as well, causing fragility that can't be detected but can create an unstable layer, which can lead to an avalanche with the slightest provocation.

Then the media interviewed the grieving relatives of those killed in the avalanche and followed up with the blame stories. They gathered experts who faulted snowmobile drivers or sloppy maintenance. Politicians spoke about the need to consider banning snowmobiles during certain times of the year.

Essentially, every national media organization in the country had a producer or reporter in Pennsylvania. After the avalanche story ran its course, a group of reporters heard a local radio report about a young woman who'd broken into a women's health clinic and escaped with stolen fetal remains. This local story likely never would've been noticed by the national media, but the clinic was only forty-seven minutes away. And once some reporters told their editors that other newspapers and cable channels were heading to Thebes, they were afraid of missing out.

The previous month an abortion doctor had been beaten into a coma outside his home in Tennessee. For days, news media reported anti-abortion violence was skyrocketing throughout the country. Experts called for new hate crime laws, increased buffer zones around clinics, and the closure of pro-life health clinics. However, when the doctor awoke, he said he had been beaten by an angry neighbor over the location of a fence.

But they just knew this story about a young girl stealing remains from an abortion clinic had legs. They could feel it. The swarm descended on Thebes County.

PAUL SAT IN A diner thinking about the Prince girls and staring at his blank computer screen when the first news van passed. Then another. He looked up. There were few sickening feelings in the world like a reporter seeing news vans rush by for unknown reasons.

Paul paid his bill and ran to his car, the thrill of the hunt making his limbs feel electric. As he pulled out of the driveway, another news van drove past. He followed it. They couldn't be there for the Prince story, could they? That was just a follow-up. He tuned in to the local news station, whose anchor predicted overcast gray days and snarling traffic in a pleasant baritone.

The van he was following was from Philadelphia, but he saw another one parked on Main Street with New York license plates. What was going on?

Then he heard it: an anti-abortionist nut had broken into a women's clinic and stolen biological materials. Yup. That was enough to set off a media rush. He heard the district attorney had scheduled a press conference for the morning about the crime. He went back to his hotel, called the police, and they sent over their press release, which said they had yet to apprehend anyone for the crime at the clinic. He called the district attorney's office, which emailed their media advisory for the following day's 8:00 a.m. press conference.

He texted Nanzi that a national media story was brewing, and she responded by saying he should write the Prince story and then attend the presser in the morning.

He lay down but couldn't sleep. He texted Robicheaux.

Paul: Hey, got a minute.
   Tom: sup
   Paul: Went to the Prince funeral. Shit got real . . . Family stuff.
Ugly.

Tom: You lucky bastard. What happened?

Paul: Is family drama really news though? I don't wanna hurt these people on the worst day of their lives.

Tom: When did you get a soul?

Paul: Ha. Srsly.

Tom: Family of politicians. Fair game.

Paul: Not sure.

Tom: Ah. I think I understand. Is she hot?

Paul: Not about that.

Tom: So she is?

Paul: Something just feels wrong about it.

Tom: Dude, u need a big story. Ur on thin ice. Don't develop a conscience now.

Paul got out of bed and drove without direction under faltering street-lights and wondered where the few vehicles he encountered were heading at such an odd hour. He played a game he'd read about in a book once, creating emotional backstories for each pair of headlights.

As he turned into one neighborhood, his headlights illuminated a committee of black vultures gathered around a fawn's carcass on the road-side. So intent on their lifeless prey, their busy beaks didn't cease tearing as he drove within inches of them.

Bzzzz.

Nancy texted asking when to expect his story. He tossed his phone onto the passenger seat and watched his hometown pass by. There was something great about driving in a car. For at least a little while he could be all about the destination. He could forget where he was or even who he was. But when driving aimlessly, there was no place worse.

He found himself driving past the cul-de-sac where the Princes lived. A BMW sat in the driveway. After wandering for a few more minutes, he found himself back in front of that two-story colonial with three windows across and a half-acre of lawn in front.

A light illuminated the front room, the only one on the block. He considered knocking to ask for an interview despite the late hour but thought it would set the Princes on edge, and they wouldn't speak with him. After passing twice, his eyelids grew heavy, and his jaw strained with yawns, so he parked under a darkened streetlight in front of the Princes' house at 1:37 a.m.

He reclined his seat, figuring he could rest and request an interview with the family first thing in the morning. He closed his eyes, so he didn't see the dark figure emerge from the door of the Princes' house.

Though his eyes were closed, Paul noticed the motion sensor lights over the garage illuminate the front yard. He sat up and saw her across the lawn, peering into the darkness directly at him.

Crap!

He recognized Izzy immediately. She was wearing blue shorts, a baggy black sweatshirt, and red slippers. She stepped toward his car.

He wanted to race away. Why the hell had he even gone there? He searched his pockets frantically for his keys as she got even closer, leaning forward.

"Hello?" she called out into the darkness, her voice faltering.

Desperate, Paul arched his hips to search his pockets and heard a jangle. Ugh! The keys had been in the ignition the entire time. She stood at the edge of the driveway, just feet from his car. No escape. He sighed in surrender, turned the key to accessory, and lowered the passenger window.

"Izzy?"

"Who's there?" she said, her weight shifting to her back foot. Squinting.

"It's, um, Paul," he said while pulling the key out and stuffing his phone and notepad into his pockets and stepping out. "It's Paul Barnes. We went to—"

"Paul?" she said. "What are you doing here?"

"I'm a journalist with the San Francisco Reporter, and I'm—"

"Oh my Go . . ." She sank against a telephone pole, her face in her hands. "You're here about Anne, right? Did you see her?"

"Um, I saw her at the church, but . . ."

"Oh, no, no, no," she said, her hands in her hair. She retreated through the grass and collapsed on the front steps.

"Iz, I'm sorry this is happening," he said, getting out of his car and following her up the walkway. "I'm sorry I . . ." He didn't know how to continue.

She looked up at him, her wild hair spilling over her eyes. She tilted her head and bit her bottom lip as if figuring something out. "OK, Paul," she said, "I'm going to be honest with you for some odd reason. I'm having the worst week of my life, and—"

"I'm sorry," Paul said. The first rule of journalism was never to interrupt when a source was speaking, and he surprised himself by breaking it—and meaning it. "If there's anything I can do to help . . ."

She forced a laugh. "A million people have said those words to me in the past few days. And I've said it to other people in the past too. The funny thing is, we wait to offer our help until there's nothing anyone can do. And now Anne's doing the most Anne thing she's ever done, and I . . ." She went silent, searching for the right word, and then slumped. Paul wanted to reach out. Izzy had always been so full of life, excited about anything and everything, but the young woman who sat crumpled on the front steps of her mother's house had changed. Life had done that to her, and he had helped.

It occurred to him that she didn't know he'd written the original story about her father, probably because the Associated Press had run the story nationwide without his byline. She had no idea he had anything to do with it.

"This is all my fault," she said. "All of it."

"No, it's not," he assured her.

"I couldn't have been more awful to Susan Doyle. Awful. What I said . . . what I did . . ." She searched for the word and settled once again on "awful." No matter what Susan had done, she said she never should have turned her back on her.

Izzy explained that when Susan moved to Pennsylvania after law school, she didn't have family. She'd grown up as a foster child. After she started working in the district attorney's office, she had spent holidays with the Prince family and even slept over on occasion. The three of them—Anne, Izzy, and Susan—had microwaved popcorn and watched movies all night. Sometimes Susan went to church with Anne on Sundays. "We thought of her like a sister," Izzy said.

Paul had never considered Izzy's pain when writing the story. He often saw the people in his stories as characters, not real in the sense that they actually existed outside of his story. When speaking to people, he just waited for the quote, the one that would make editors smile.

As Izzy continued talking, Paul remembered a story he'd written about a single mother of three on public assistance who had lost her home in a fire. His editors loved it. The woman had dropped gem after gem, an unwitting quote machine.

Afterwards, Paul forgot about the family. Two months later that same woman approached him in the street holding out her hand, asking for a dollar. Instead of giving one to her, he wrote a follow-up piece accusing the Department of Welfare of dropping the ball. His editors loved it. He never did give her that dollar. From time to time he worried about why he wasn't more worried about such people. Was some vital synapse disconnected? Was some piece of his brain that most other people had missing? Or maybe it wasn't a real piece. Maybe others were just faking all those feelings of empathy and connection. Maybe they wanted to feel it so badly that they created such feelings to delude themselves.

Paul was lost in his own thoughts, but Izzy's words finally broke through. "Susan may not have even went for an abortion if I hadn't been so awful to her, and then Anne wouldn't have done . . . the most Anne-ish thing ever."

What?

Paul stood up straight. Susan Doyle had an abortion? He nearly pulled out his notepad. Instead, he stepped forward. All his uncertainty and angst vanished. His exhaustion? Gone. He had a story. With legs. He could feel it. He clicked on the recording app on his phone.

He had to play it cool, not scare her off. Let her tell him everything. One thing he had learned as a journalist was people wanted to tell their story. They wanted to reveal all the grimy details. Something inside humans desired to be understood and consoled. As a journalist, sometimes he merely had to be present and not scare them off while they played with their self-destruct button.

The two of them sat so still that the motion detector light timed out. Izzy waved her hand, and it illuminated the yard once again.

"Paul," she said, looking up. "I haven't prayed in years, but just now, right inside the living room, I prayed for a miracle, and then you pulled up. I prayed for the first time since I was a kid, and your headlights filled the room. I mean, for a second I thought maybe God was giving me a sign or something." She laughed and looked at him to see if he thought she was crazy, but he kept his face noncommittal. "And I go outside and it's . . . a reporter, no offense."

"None taken."

"I mean, I could sure use a miracle right now, and either you're it or the universe is having a big laugh at my expense" she said, rolling her eyes as if she knew she sounded insane. She stood. "Paul, if I invite you in, can you just be my friend and not a reporter?"

He nodded but didn't turn off his recorder

23

Izzy asked Paul if he wanted a sweet tea or water. He didn't want either, but when his phone vibrated with a message, he asked for a water and took the opportunity to check his phone.

Nanzi had sent two messages: "Story in asap!!!" and "What's going on with you, Paul?"

He stuffed it back in his pocket.

Two couches sat facing each other across a coffee table. He perused the bookshelf on the wall. Law books, Tolstoy, Nietzsche, Dickens, Sartre, Dostoyevsky, G. K. Chesterton, C. S. Lewis, Dean Koontz, Jane Austen, and Maeve Binchy.

Izzy walked in and handed him a glass. Her dog slippers with whiskers seemed like an artifact of her happy past, at odds with her present. She sat across from him in the love seat. Being inside had changed something, and she forced a smile. He remained silent.

In Paul's experience, there were different kinds of silence. One where people couldn't think of what to say because no word could bridge the distance between them. The other was when both people wanted to avoid talking about the thing that desperately needed to be talked about.

Robicheaux had taught Paul that awkward silence was a journalist's best friend because people felt the need to fill silences, and reporters made a living when people did. Paul leaned forward, his elbows on his knees, staring.

Izzy laughed and threw up her hands. "So, I'm guessing you're here about Anne? How did you even find out?"

The question flummoxed him. He quickly reviewed his options and landed on scaring her. "Izzy, reporters find out everything. I suspect many more journalists are coming. My advice is to turn out the front light, and

79

don't speak to anyone. Me? I just want you and Anne to get your side of the story out. I'm on your side."

"Thank you so much, Paul," she said. "This is so bad. She really stepped in it this time. You know how she is."

"I remember," he said. "Soooo, why don't you start from the beginning?"

She inhaled, and he held his breath. She told him everything, including up to the moment Anne texted her from St. Stephen the Martyr's Parish about the police outside. He realized that when he said he'd seen her at the church, Izzy had thought he meant that night.

So, no other journalists were aware that Anne Prince, daughter of the deceased district attorney and niece of the new district attorney, had stolen the fetal remains of her dead father's aborted child and was surrounded by police. In a church! His pulse raced, and his mind sought an excuse to get to the church, but Izzy continued talking.

"Is this more than you want to know?" she asked at one point. "Am I talking too much?"

"No," he said. "I like hearing your voice."

"I think I talk a lot when I'm scared," she said, then looked up at the ceiling. "Well, I'm plenty scared right now. My dad always said I was like china in a bull shop. Like my mom. Maybe he was right."

He wanted to tell her he didn't think she was like her mother, but he had to go.

Stay, a voice inside his head erupted.

Stay? What? He had to go. The biggest story of his career was right outside. The chance to show all of them he was the best.

Stay.

That's when Izzy dropped the bomb that Anne intended to have a funeral for their "brother" at the church. She used air quotes when she referred to her "brother" and placed her hands on either side of her head. "This is so bad. It's literally going to kill my mother. I mean, like, literally," she said. "I honestly don't know what to do."

She stood, crossed over to the couch, and sat next to him. He wanted to help her. He wanted to . . .

Bzzz. His phone vibrated.

"You can check it," she said, wiping her eyes. "I'm sorry to be so . . . I don't even know."

He pulled out his phone.

Nanzi: "National news occurring, and I have a reporter missing and NO STORY. Ramifications."

"What can I do?" Izzy asked, her face helpless and open.

This girl who always had people lining up to be her friend, who giggled her way through life, wiped away tears with her sleeve.

"Izzy . . ." he said.

Bzzzz.

"Izzy, I'm . . . um . . . Listen, Iz . . . I feel somewhat responsible . . . The story . . ."

Bzzzzzz.

"Do you have to take that?" she asked.

"Iz, I'm sorry," he said. "I have to go."

Stay.

She wiped her eyes and stepped back, feigning nonchalance. "Yeah, that's fine."

"Izzy, I'm um, going to the church to speak to Anne. You wanna come?" He thought her presence might give him a better chance of scoring the interview.

Her eyes retreated. "I don't think so. My mom is upstairs. And I think no matter how this turns out she'll need me . I don't think I've been a great daughter. Heck, I don't think I've been a great anything. For so long I kinda thought everything was about me, so maybe this is what I'm supposed to do for now. Anyway, it's what Anne asked me to do." She stepped back from him and leaned against the wall.

He stepped past her to the door. Izzy followed. "Paul, I've learned that I supposedly don't trust people enough to ask for help or something. And I'm still not good at it, but hey, you're supposed to be my miracle and all, so I just wanted to tell you that things didn't go . . . as I thought they would. High school came easily for me. Everything came easily back then. Anyway, I came home from college, you know. It didn't work out. Nothing worked out like the way I thought it would. I didn't even work out the way I thought I would . . ."

"None of us did," Paul said, looking down.

She looked around as if searching for the words in the air above his face. "Anne . . . she's a lot, you know. Don't get me wrong. She's amazing, and I love her. She stood by me when I had the eating disorder. Funny thing is, she didn't understand it at all. She just wanted to tell me to eat more. Like WTH, Iz, right? But she never did. Every meal she'd ask what I wanted. It didn't matter to her what she wanted, you know. Sometimes I'd pick a meal she'd hate just to be a bitch. I know, it sounds awful. And sometimes I'd catch her counting my bites. At the time it drove me bananas, you know. I'd call her all sorts of names and storm away, and she'd just come up later and act like I hadn't just completely lost it on her and ask if I wanted to go out for ice cream or something. She's relentless and, like, so totally unsubtle. Obviously. It drove me crazy, but it's kind of nice when I think about it, you know what I mean? It's nice to have someone in your life who when you need them isn't all about themselves, you know?"

"It would be," Paul said, opening the door.

Stay.

He moved within inches of her and squeezed past her in the doorway. He tried to look away and failed.

Bzzzzz.

This could be the biggest story of his career, rocket him right to the top over all those Ivy League journalism school snobs. He could leave San Francisco and go . . . where? Chicago? New York? A place where editors appreciated real journalism.

"I've really gotta go." He stepped through the doorway. She looked after him, leaning against the door, the side of her face against the frame.

Stay.

He turned, halfway down the steps. "Izzy, did you call your uncle? He's the DA. He might be able to help."

She bit her lower lip and hesitated.

"Call him." It was the only kindness he could extend.

While walking to his car, he texted Nanzi and Robicheaux. "Story getting deep . . . dead DA's daughter stole fetal remains from women's health clinic where her Dad's mistress had an abortion. She's holing herself up in a church surrounded by police. Her uncle is now the DA."

"You're the luckiest bastard in the world," Robicheaux replied. "Take the bitch down."

He quickly texted Robicheaux separately: "Dude, you're in a group text with Nancy, and you just said 'bitch.'"

No response.

Nanzi responded in the group chat: "Great job, Paul. Get me story asap. Tom, let's talk."

Izzy waved to him as he pulled away. He tried not to look at her.

Stay.

25

PAUL LUCKED INTO THE three police officers not seeing him as he pulled into the church parking lot. He'd parked behind the rectory where the priest lived and didn't even notice the police until he walked around the side of the church. There they were, all badges, guns, and crewcuts in conversation, thankfully facing the street. He backed up, holding his breath.

He walked around the stone church, pulling on each door. Locked. On the far side he pulled on a wooden door with a circular top, but it didn't budge. About ten yards farther he discovered some cement steps with a metal railing descending to a green metal door. He took the uneven steps carefully in the darkness, holding onto the wobbly railing. He pulled on the handle, and the door screamed with rust. He dashed in and pulled it closed behind him and looked around as he waited for his eyes to adjust. His heart hammered in his chest.

An exit sign on the far side of the room illuminated just enough so he could see two green metallic lockers to his right. Hanging inside were red-and-white religious garments. He was not Catholic, but they looked . . . ceremonial.

As his eyes adjusted, he made out stairs ascending to his left and a hallway to his right that opened to a large empty room with stacked metal chairs. He was trying to decide which way to go when a cone of light illuminated the outside stairwell. Paul looked out the window and saw a pair of black shoes descending the outside steps. The police had heard him!

He looked for an escape. Down the hall or up the stairs? He leapt toward the stairs and took them two at a time, thinking that at any moment he'd be enveloped in light and thrown into handcuffs or look up to see a priest grimacing at him from the top of the stairwell. Four steps from the top, he heard the big metal door slam behind him. He froze.

Move and risk a sound or stay still and hope the police didn't look up the stairwell? Holding his breath, he looked down the stairs to see it illuminated. The light turned up the stairs and would reach him within seconds. On his toes, he leapt up the final few steps.

He turned the corner and stepped to his right with his back to the wall just as the intense light reflected off the wall in front of him. He tensed. He heard footsteps on the stairs, coming up slowly. Paul looked around for an escape.

To his left he heard muffled, distant voices. To get there he'd have to cross in front of the light, so Paul peeled off the wall and ran into a room on the right.

The flashlight went out. Paul stopped moving and listened. He didn't hear anyone moving away. He suspected the officer was standing in the darkened stairwell listening for him. Paul didn't dare move because he couldn't see even a foot in front of him. He heard two people talking in the church but not what they were saying. It was a man's voice and a woman's voice. Even though he couldn't make out her words, he knew Anne's voice.

He closed his eyes and then opened them. In the darkness he saw a large number of cabinets and drawers and a sink. He crept forward and listened.

A scrape? His entire being focused on listening. A footfall? The police officer was ascending the stairs. Paul had to act. Holding up his phone, he turned it on, and the dim light revealed an open door on the far side of the room. He turned off his phone and took four quick steps forward. There he saw a stairwell with a low ceiling and stone walls, barely tall enough for a grown man, leading upwards.

He slipped inside and climbed on his toes. As he reached the top he turned around to see if the light followed. Nothing.

He turned his attention to the spacious room in front of him with a large stained-glass window facing the entrance of the church. He found himself in a choir loft littered with cardboard boxes and a nativity set with a stable, wise men, shepherds, and the baby Jesus laid out on the floor like a holy mosh pit. He crept into the carpeted space and crouched as he neared the balcony railing. He lifted his eyes just above the rail and peered down into the sanctuary to see two silhouettes facing each other in the pews. It was Anne and the priest, the same short chubby man from the funeral.

Anne laughed, which surprised him. Panic, perhaps? He had expected tears, not this. Paul lowered himself to the carpet with his back to the balcony. He found himself smiling too and staring at a stained-glass window depicting a man being stoned by two men with large stones aimed at his head. Weirdly, the guy on the ground seemed cool with it.

Paul didn't consider himself a Christian although he was probably technically a Baptist if one could be a Baptist without actually believing anything. His family attended services on Christmas or Easter in his childhood, but he could tell from an early age it was just a place they went once or twice a year, like the Department of Motor Vehicles. At some point even that stopped.

He huddled in the farthest corner behind several boxes and began typing his story into his phone. He dimmed the brightness, and every shift and movement seemed so loud, but the two voices continued speaking, clearly unaware of his presence, until the priest left at around 4:30 a.m. After finishing his story, Paul texted Robicheaux, asking him to add a comment or a statement from the police and something from the clinic. At 5:27 a.m., he submitted the story. Robicheaux said the clinic had issued a press release, so they'd add quotes from the release, and other reporters would add details from police that Paul couldn't access from his current position.

He put his phone on vibrate and tried to fall asleep but mostly stared at a large tree on the front lawn of the church. He reclined straight back and marveled at how the tree's branches twisted themselves outward and upward in various directions to receive sunlight.

Right before Paul fell asleep, Robicheaux texted him: "This is a story of national interest. A career maker, my friend."

25

At 6:09 a.m. Eastern Time, the website of the San Francisco Reporter published the following piece.

> Police are surrounding a Catholic Church in Thebes County, Pennsylvania, due to an ongoing incident in which a young woman, who is a suspect in a crime involving stealing biohazardous material from a women's clinic where abortions are performed, has declared sanctuary inside.
>
> Despite local police saying they're attempting to locate the suspect, the *San Francisco Reporter* can verify that the suspect is Anne Prince, daughter of former Senate candidate Edward Prince who passed away last week in the hotel room of Assistant District Attorney Susan Doyle. Isabella Prince, Anne's sister, confirmed that the Prince family believes Doyle was in a sexual relationship with their father because he was found in her room in his underwear, as the *San Francisco Reporter* reported last week. Just one day after Prince's funeral, Susan Doyle was rushed to Mercy Hospital after suffering complications from a surgical procedure to terminate a pregnancy at the Elizabeth Blackwell Women's Clinic. A YouTube video posted earlier this week and seen by hundreds of people, including the Princes, showed Doyle being transported from the clinic to the hospital.
>
> After seeing the video, Anne Prince, according to her sister Isabelle, entered the clinic with the intent of retrieving the remains of the fetus, which she called "her brother."
>
> Anne Prince reportedly left the clinic with one sample of fetal remains with the intent of holding a funeral Mass.
>
> Prince entered the church yesterday at around 10:00 a.m. with police pursuing on foot. Reportedly Fr. Peter Quinn, the pastor of the church, asked the police not to enter the building, claiming he needed to offer her "spiritual guidance."

Visitors and parishioners are currently being turned away from the grounds of St. Stephen the Martyr's Church in Eagleville while authorities decide on a strategy to end the standoff.

Blackwell Clinic Director Allie Schine called for the arrest of the suspect and said this incident was an indication of the rising tide of anti-abortion violence seen throughout our country over the past few years.

The current district attorney of Thebes County is Anne Prince's uncle, Milton Prince, who was appointed to the position after his brother's death. Some are already calling for him to recuse himself in this situation. His office did not respond to inquiries . . .

The site highlighted a link to the Blackwell Clinic's press release.

Comments from the *San Francisco Reporter* story:

1. So, is he going to let her off? Is the law for everyone or only a select few? Prosecute this bitch.

2. I'm a bird watcher. I have seen mother birds return to a barren nest crying over their dead children. I can't help but think this young girl felt the same way when she did this.

3. Pass the popcorn please . . .

26

A CATASTROPHE. HOLY HELL, the 8:00 a.m. presser careened off the rails. The pack of wolves drew early blood from the new DA and pounced. On national television.

Less than nine hours later, someone named "freakduh69" on YouTube published video of Milton Prince's first attempt at dealing with the press and interspersed National Geographic video of whales tossing a seal around for play and tearing its bloated corpse.

Yes, that bad.

That morning, Milton left his home, sent a call from Izzy to voicemail, and listened to self-affirmation CDs on the drive. He spoke the words of his memorized statement about being tough on lawbreakers and prosecuting those found guilty of this "shocking crime" to the fullest extent of the law. Easy enough, right?

And then reality struck.

Upon arriving at the courthouse, his stomach turned over when he saw dozens of reporters, including recognizable faces from cable news channels, crowding near the courthouse door. When the pack charged toward him, his first instinct was to run.

He wanted headlines, but he had never expected national attention. Had he missed something? He'd planned to speak with Walter/Alan before the presser, but the reporters pressed up against him, demanding he answer questions. Milton stepped back against the hood of his black Audi and assured himself he could handle this. No problem. He'd planned to do it on the courthouse steps, but why not right there?

The situation spiraled after he finished his memorized statement about working closely with police and bringing the wrongdoers to justice. He actually used the word "wrongdoers." Feeling good, Milton decided to answer a few questions. When a young brunette woman with a messy bun and squinty eyes looked over her glasses at him and asked if there were any injuries reported in the clinic, he said no, but not wanting to sound uncommunicative, he continued on about the importance of enforcing laws that protected abortion clinic workers at abortion facilities.

The squinty-eyed messy bun's face recoiled. Uh-oh. What had he said? Out of the corner of his eye, he saw Walter/Alan wince. Had he said something wrong? The day before the kid had instructed him to say "biological materials," and he had remained so focused on that, though he forgot to call it a "women's health clinic" and never ever an "abortion clinic."

Hands shot up, and he looked to Walter/Alan, who stared blankly back. The kid had told him the day before that once the presser began. he couldn't be seen as needing help.

"Sir, you referred to the women's clinic as an 'abortion facility.' Where does that description come from?" one reporter yelled from the back.

"Isn't that just anti-women rhetoric?" a blogger with purple hair asked.

"Why are you attacking the victim of this crime by not calling it a women's health clinic?" a muscular man in a tight suit asked. "Isn't that what you're doing?"

Milton grew wide eyed as the questions pummeled him over whether he would renounce his party's anti-abortion position or if the anti-abortion movement had grown increasingly violent and required further legal restrictions to ensure the safety of women and clinic workers.

"Sir, are you coordinating with police about the standoff at St. Stephen the Martyr's Church?" asked an obese balding man in jeans and a button-down shirt with his sleeves rolled up.

"I'm um . . ." Milton looked around with the most obvious "oh crap" face" ever seen on camera. "I'm um . . . in constant communication with police on many matters."

The journalists all chattered over each other. They'd read the piece that morning from the *San Francisco Reporter* by Paul Barnes and assumed Milton would recuse himself or say it didn't matter that the suspect was his niece. Something. Acknowledge the giant elephant crapping in the room!

"Sir, are you even aware the suspect is named Anne Prince? She is your niece, is she not?" This was the part of the YouTube video where the whale gripped the seal in its mouth, twirled it, and tossed it forty feet in the air.

Prince shot up a flare of desperation to Walter/Alan, who stared at his phone and nodded urgently to him with wide helpless eyes. Cameras rolled, and the sweat ran down Milton's cheeks. He wiped it away with his sleeve.

The questions escalated into an indecipherable chorus, but Milton attempted to speak over it, trying to sound stern and confident. His memorized phrase, "Anyone who runs afoul of the law shall not be spared and will pay a steep price for this egregious crime," came out as a string of mumbled syllables with the words "spared" and "egregious" bubbling to the surface of coherence.

A disaster. Milton excused himself and walked through the court-house doors. The journalists could be heard following and laughing on the video. Walter/Alan alternately whispered into his phone and to Milton as they walked down the hallway, through the café, and into his office.

Milton collapsed in his office chair, pulled out his phone, and saw the text from Izzy. He hadn't returned her call that morning as he prepared for the press conference. He called her back, and she tearfully told him everything. He felt sick, so sick that he considered asking Walter/Alan for a trashcan. Instead, he lay his head on his desk and concentrated on not vomiting.

Izzy said everything was her fault, but she'd just been trying to help.

"Don't 'help' anymore," Milton said. "I'll call you with updates."

He hung up and stared at the young man. "What the hell is your name again?" he asked.

"Lawrence."

"Well, Lawrence, how the hell did you let this happen?"

27

PAUL WOKE UP ON the floor confused. He scanned the room and saw boxes, stacked wreaths, and a plastic shepherd staring at him beneath a large stained-glass window.

Oh. Yeah. It all came back. He checked his phone and saw a number of texts. Izzy had texted earlier: "I called my uncle. l/m. Thanks 4 everthng."

Paul cringed.

Nancy had also texted: "Good job. Keep it up." He wondered if it had hurt her thumbs to write that.

He began to read his article on the front page of the site when an uproar from outside startled him. He crawled over to the window and peered out, certain nobody below could see him. The sun had risen somewhere but offered little light. In the surrounding grayness, he saw about two dozen people in front of the church holding signs that said things like "Get your rosaries off my ovaries" or "My body, my choice." Wow. That was fast. Police had already established a perimeter with yellow tape. In the rectory parking lot, Paul saw four news vans parked around his car.

He crawled back from the edge and peered over the balcony. A few candles flickered near the altar, illuminating the Virgin Mary statue. He panicked when he didn't immediately see Anne. He was about to stand and look for her when he heard a noise. A whisper? No. A page turning?

He spotted her sitting in a large windowsill, reading, her knees up and her coat draped over her like a blanket. Just outside, the crowd of protesters stood framed in the large window.

One man holding a sign pointed her out, and soon a majority were pointing and holding up their phones while screaming epithets such as "Nazi" and "Zealot!"

Anne didn't react. She was sitting just yards from a volcano of anger but seemed unaware or unfazed. Paul wondered what she was reading.

"Criminal! Criminal! Criminal!" The crowd had settled on a chant, and some tossed small rocks. Many crashed harmlessly against stone, but others clinked against the window. Anne didn't look their way.

Their movement outside became erratic, frenzied. They recorded their own rage with their phones and took pictures of her in the window, their phones dancing like fireflies in the gray morning. Some bent over, searching the ground for rocks. The trees limbs swayed in the wind like children seeking attention, but Anne remained still, only turning the pages now and again. Three police officers gathered in front of the crowd, their voices rising above the swirling wind outside. They sounded like ghosts. He couldn't make out their words, just their pleading tones. That's when Paul understood the police had no power over the situation and were simply trying to manage the crowd. For the first time he feared for Anne's safety. She too must have heard their rage and the whine of the undermanned police force. She had to know there was at least a possibility, if not a likelihood, of things going bad. But there she sat. Still. Serene. Reading.

His phone buzzed. A text from Izzy: "Some miracle you turned out to be."

He didn't respond. He sank back into invisibility under the railing. He wanted to explain himself but didn't think he could make her understand. She'd placed her faith in him, and he had used her. That was the heart of it, wasn't it? He consoled himself that any reporter would've done much worse by Anne. Much worse. He told himself many things.

Comments on YouTube:

1. This asshat was appointed DA. This is his first press conference, and he gets absolutely shellacked. Hilarious.

2. The look in his eyes! It's where hope and pride go to die.

3. Is that sweat or is God pissing on him?

4. Must-watch video of the day!

5. There is no happiness where there is no wisdom, and there is no wisdom but in submission to God

6. Big words are always punished, and those were some big words coming out of his mouth.

7. This guy just got served. Hardcore.

8. They say, "Proud men in old age learn to be wise." This guy could live until he's 500 and still be stupid as sh#t

9. Pride goeth before the fall.

28

FRANK WHIPPLE ENTERED MILTON's office without announcing himself. Milton, seated at his desk, looked up. The man's belly hung over his belt, and the bottom of his blue shirt hung out on one side, untucked. On his phone, Whipple waved a finger at Milton, asking for a moment as if Milton had interrupted him.

"You need to get on that," Whipple said and waved his fingers in the air again, this time signaling he needed a pen. Milton glanced around for a pen as Whipple came around and backed into him, nudging him with his round hip. The nudge quickly elevated into an all-out assault by Whipple's butt that sent Milton scrambling out of his chair to avoid contact with the fat man.

Milton stood by the side of his desk as Whipple squeezed his girth into the seat with a grunt.

"Well, you put on quite a show," Whipple said after hanging up.

Milton closed his eyes, the embarrassment of the day still too fresh.

"Hey!" Whipple yelled. "I'm talking to you, Mr. DA."

"Oh, sorry, I thought you were still talking on the phone," Milton lied.

Whipple closed his flip phone with his thick fingers and leaned back in the chair. "Sit," he said, pointing to the other side of his desk. Milton realized Whipple had never even used the pen. It was merely a blatant alpha power play.

In response, Milton placed his hands on the edge of the desk and attempted to tower over Whipple, but he still felt small and defeated.

Whipple leaned back and smiled, spittle at the corner of his mouth. "Can I be honest with you, Milton? If you don't want the truth, I get it. But if you don't want to hear it, tell me to get the hell out because I only have one setting, and it's no bullshit. So?"

Milton's face flushed. Yes, he was being talked to like this. He pressed his hands into the desk and stared at a little one-inch black ink dot on his desk that he'd never noticed before. He fixated on the tiny dark mark. Had his brother drawn it? As he stared at it, Whipple's voice seemed to come from a greater distance. The blackness had been colored outside the line just a little bit on the top, and that irregularity captured his eye. Milton obsessed over the blackness. Had Edward drawn it while listening to someone like Whipple?

"Milton, Milton, you want the truth?" Whipple asked.

"Yes," he said without looking up.

"This moment is a godsend. A godsend, I tell you. If you come down hard on your niece, you'll become a legend. Milton Prince will be seen as the baddest mofo who prosecuted his own niece. Don't mess with him, am I right? Criminals will crap their Wranglers. Political opponents will avoid your stare in the halls." He sniggered, a guttural gurgle.

Milton stared into the blackness. The dot seemed almost three dimensional. He imagined crawling onto his desk, stretching the dot out with his hands, and diving in. Just diving right in to the black and pulling it closed behind him.

"Milton, the best move you can make is to send the officers into the church and drag the dear girl out by her ponytail. I hate to be crass, but this will assure your victory. I've spoken to the pro-life lunatics. They don't want nothing to do with this crapfest. You believe that? The fanatics think she makes them look like fanatics. Ha! And the pro-choicers obviously despise her with an ungodly passion. This girl has no friends. She's the perfect enemy."

Milton winced.

"Look, I get it, Milton. She's family. Just prosecute her, toss her in jail, and release her early for good behavior with an agreement to Skype some expensive shrink while she eats oatmeal at home in her pajamas. Soon nobody will even remember her. But they'll remember you as the badass who tossed his niece in the clink. The main thing is the visual of the police dragging this bitch out. No matter what, you get in that shot."

Milton could hardly see Whipple anymore. The corner of his vision blackened, and Whipple's massive body seemed smaller and farther away. But his voice still resonated. Every jab of a syllable, every sickening sound of his smacking lips.

"Look," Whipple continued, "I know when you took this job you wanted to do something good. Reform, right? That's your favorite word, isn't it?

I'm thinking in the special election we put that on yard signs. 'Milton Price: Reform.' Don't lock me in, but I'm ruminating. You're not a law-and-order guy like your brother. I get that. You're a bleeding heart. I like that about you. But to do good, you need power. Listen to me; most people consider themselves good. But here's the thing: they just don't have the opportunity to do anything else. When you're meek, you're not good. You're just power-less. A rabbit doesn't have to decide not to bite people. A dog makes that decision. That's why we invite dogs into our houses, and we eat rabbits.

"What I'm saying is that in order to be good, you need a choice. You need to be able to affect change. Otherwise you're nothing. Milton, I'm talk-ing up in the clouds here. I'll bring it back into orbit for you. Let's say you don't drag her out, and she stays in the church for a week or two. Well, the church doesn't want her there because nobody can get in, which means the collection baskets stay empty. And nothing pisses off the Church like empty collection baskets. The normals want her arrested because she broke the damn law, and they'll rant that the only reason she's not in jail is because she's your niece. If you allow this to continue, the anger against her will only grow. You won't be helping her. You'll be making her the world's best-known criminal. She's already on all the cable news channels. Drag her out, indict her, and this is a one- or two-day story. If you don't go after her with everything you have at your disposal as the DA of this county, well yay, Uncle Milty. It'll make for a great Thanksgiving "pass the damn cranberries and stuffing" moment won't it? But it'll be a great scandal, and you'll be voted out as sure as the pilgrims screwed the Indians. And what happens to the rest of the county? You know the first damn thing the other party will do when they win; they'll fire everyone who works here and replace them with their own people. Everyone you work with, everyone you pass in the hall, will be out of a job because you want to be the cool uncle. What about their families, Milton? Do you give a damn about them?

"And holy hell, guess what happens when the other side gets the power of prosecution? Every damn Republican they can point at will be investi-gated. And they'll know where to damn well look because they're up to the same crap we are."

Milton backed away from the desk and sat heavily, his arms hanging down the sides of the chair. "Frank, I don't want to be selfish about this. I can't prioritize my own political needs above hers. I just don't know . . ."

Whipple wriggled himself out of his chair. It took a moment, his jowls quivering with the effort. He walked out into the hallway. "Everyone in here!" he yelled. "Yeah, even you, candy boy. Get the hell in here. Now."

The office crowded with dozens of workers looking at Frank and Milton and tossing questioning looks at each other, but Whipple continued speaking to Milton as if the others weren't there. "So, you say you don't want to be selfish. I'm explaining to you that not indicting . . . what's her name is the most selfish act in the history of this damn county. So, have a nice Thanksgiving while all these good people are looking for a job. That's the decision you're making. Look at their faces."

He approached one woman, "How many kids you have?"

"Three," she said.

"What are their names?"

"Timmy, June, and Mika."

"Well, you tell little Timmy and Michael they're not going to college because Milton here wants to be popular at home, OK? Call them right now, and tell them. I'm serious. All of you, take out your phones, and tell your kids college won't be in the cards, but it's OK because Milty here will be the most popular uncle of all time."

Each of them pulled out their phones, and some of them actually dialed. Others looked at the large man as if to ask "Are we really doing this?" Still others stared accusingly at Milton. They understood the stakes. They'd seen the press conference. What had been a salacious bit of gossip about the new boss had transformed instantly into Def Con 1 "Holy crap, this thing could burn us all down" kind of serious. Their eyes burned into Milton.

"Say the names of your children!" Whipple yelled.

"Mary, Bridget, Tony, Tamir, Connor, Jose, Corinne, Shannon, Shanay, Jennifer, Robbie, Tom, Shanice, Colin, Anthony . . ."

The weight of their stares pressed on Milton until he bowed his head.

"Alright, get the hell out!" Whipple said to everyone. "Close the door. Can't we get some goddamn privacy around here?"

Calming and docile, Whipple came around and patted Milton on the back. "This is the right thing to do in the long run."

"Let me speak with her first," Milton said without looking up. "I'll go in. I think she'll come out with me. That OK?"

Whipple looked at the ceiling tiles as if calculating. "You know what? I like it. You go in, and come out with her. That's the best visual of all. And if she doesn't come out, send the boys in blue to drag her out. Hold a press conference right there on the damn church steps, and announce she'll be prosecuted to the fullest extent of the law. I like it." Whipple smiled, and even his steps seemed lighter.

"Um, one thing Frank," Milton said. "What about the clinic?"

"What about it?" Whipple asked as if he'd just heard something outlandish.

Milton lifted his head. "I'm the D.A. Shouldn't we look into the charges of illegal dumping of fetal remains to show fairness?"

"Jesus, Milton," Whipple said. "Hand it off it to the damn health department. Those creampuffs don't have to run for reelection. Let them ignore it. I mean, do you want to pick a fight with the largest women's health clinic, which donates millions of dollars to the other side? Believe me, you don't want to be on their radar because they will dump five million dollars to drag you through the rectum shredder. Not only will you lose this job, your name will be smeared. That ain't the way, pal. The truth is, those bastards will destroy your life for fun. Anyway, do you wanna crucify these people because of the truckers' strike? That's not their fault. They're doing their best. Look, I know this seems big right now, but this is nothing. Nothing. But you have to deal with a lot of nothings to get to the something. The only thing is you decide what's something and what's nothing. Milton, think of all the reform you can do in that seat."

Milton decided he hated this man in front of him, this corpulent pus bomb of ambition and greed. He personified everything wrong with the system. Careful not to show it, Milton realized that if he wanted to change anything inside this rotten county, he'd have to get rid of Whipple.

How though?

He was the district attorney. He'd prosecute the fat bastard. For what? He'd find something eventually. Not now. He needed him now. He'd use Whipple for now just as Whipple was using him. But eventually, he'd turn on him.

That made him smile. A path. His plan to reform the county would continue, and the path would be right over Whipple, whose mouth continued moving, flecks of spittle coalescing in the folds of his lips.

To reform the county, he would do what Whipple said. For now. He would do anything to reform this county. But first he had to get the people on his side. He'd have to make himself so popular that he could take Whipple down and remake the system entirely.

Milton stood and walked around the desk and took back his chair.

29

When Fr. Quinn left the church the previous night after hearing Anne's confession, he wished the three officers a good night on his way back to the rectory. When he returned in the morning, every camera and light was aimed at the portly priest. They surrounded him. He shielded his eyes with his hands.

The reporters barked questions, but Fr. Quinn merely smiled. Police Chief Anthony Thomas, a tall man with a rough face, approached and asked to speak with Fr. Quinn in private—right there in front of all the cameras.

The media reported that while they could not confirm police considered the "very conservative priest" a suspect, he was, in fact, "being questioned by the authorities."

Some news reports implied Fr. Quinn may have masterminded the crime or at least been an accomplice from the beginning. The media repeatedly called thirty-one-year-old Fr. Quinn "the young priest" because he'd retained much of his youthful appearance due to his chubby cheeks and lineless face. He'd also kept his hair, a fact that surprised him because everyone in his family was bald, including his grandmother.

Some reporters interviewed parishioners who Fr. Quinn said would sometimes preach about abortion and other "culture war" issues during his homilies. One parishioner said with pursed lips that it disappointed her that such a young priest held such "right-wing views." The picture much of the media used came from Fr. Quinn's Facebook page. It showed the priest looking sidelong at the camera in a sinister way with an arched eyebrow in a way he thought comical.

Inside the rectory, Fr. Quinn assured the police chief he had no prior knowledge of anything Anne Prince had planned or done, and he believed she would surrender after a funeral Mass in the morning. He also told them all were welcome in the church, and the police were the ones escalating it into a standoff.

When the chief came out he told his officers not to allow anyone else in the church. Some suspected he had intentionally made it into a standoff to force the archdiocese to act. Others, however, more charitably believed Chief Thomas didn't want to place police in the role of questioning people's intentions as they entered a church. It was also likely he believed that if the protesters were allowed inside the church, violence would be inevitable.

One television anchor interviewed a constitutional expert who suggested that the Church's tax-exempt status would be endangered the longer the situation dragged on.

30

THE LATE-MORNING SUNLIGHT SHONE through the rectangular basement windows right onto Todd Dooley's face. He rolled over but still felt the heat on his back. With a grunt, he reached for his phone on the small table next to his bed. Four other regulars were already in the chatroom buzzing excitedly. He rubbed his eyes and focused. Holy crap! Something was occurring right there in Thebes. He rubbed his entire face to wake himself. He hadn't shaved in what, two, three days?

Todd sat on the edge of his bed with his bare feet on the cold tile. He stared into his phone. "Myfisttoyourface" had posted a link to the story.

Todd felt the color flush from his face as he saw the name "Anne Prince."

"I know this fascist bitch," Todd typed into his phone, pulling his long black hair out of his face. He climbed the stairs in his boxers and T-shirt. "Mom?" he yelled before stepping out of the basement, just to ensure nobody was home. Silence. Good. He sat at his father's kitchen table and typed: "She was always stuck up and acted like the world owed her something." The others asked him about her.

Tdooley: She was my year. Miss perfect. Super Christian type. Stuck up. I'm pretty sure she hated me.

Sandybeaches: You think everyone hates you. You're paranoid.

Tdooley: Ha. I'm the opposite of paranoid. My worst fear is nobody's plotting against me because that would mean I'm not doing my job. I'm just hoping leadership moves on this thing. I'd love to get active. Even if they don't, I'm probably heading over anyway. I'm literally less than a mile away.

Sandybeaches: Not to worry. I think leadership has been great.

Iledandbled: I don't even hope people are great anymore. Maybe I should start assuming everyone I come in contact with is

101

a total fraud and poser. That way I won't be disappointed and miserable. Well, I'll still probably be miserable but not disappointed. That's progress, right?

Sandybeaches: Oh, it was Todd's birthday a few days ago. Happy birthday tdooley.

Tdooley: Thanks. My parents threw me a little birthday party, and it was just pathetic. Like they still think I'm four. They had a cake, and the three of them sang. My grandma came over, and the whole thing just devastated me, how pathetic we all were. I had to lie down for three hours.

Sandybeaches: Hahahaha. Did you get anything good?

Tdooley: Gift cards! Oh, and lectures from my dad and grandma about how I'm "smart as a whip" and should be looking for a job. And I'm like, "Yeah, the economy needs its worker bees. Let's feed the beast." They don't even get it!!!

Scranton20: "Smart as a whip." Is that term a callback to slavery?

Tdooley: Grandmother. So yeah. Probably.

Sandybeaches: I'm excited.

Tdooley: I remember my first event. We were canceling some fascist dude speaking at Temple University. The guy, a little Indian dude (actually from India), was set to talk about abortion and he was all like pro-Handmaids Tale right down the line. But this guy, I'll give him credit, this guy gets out of his car, and he's faced with 80 people in masks. And he's a little guy. Nothing to him. But he acts like it's just Tuesday, and we aren't even there. He just starts walking right toward us. I'll admit, I give the guy props. Nine guys out of ten don't get out of that car. Hell, 99 guys out of 100. But this guy did. I can't remember his name right now, but I was impressed. Anyway, this little dude marches right toward us. And I'll be honest, a bunch of us just got out of his way. I mean, just nobody expected the pure balls of the guy. And he walks through us like a knife through butter. Until this one dude. Huge guy. Hoodie. Mask and sunglasses. The whole thing. He just stands there and shakes his head like saying, "Don't do it. Don't even think about walking past me." Now, this little fella, he pauses. Just a little bit. Like, just a tiny hitch in his step. And it was like the spell was broken. Everyone snaps out of it. We all start yelling and getting up on him, calling him a Nazi, like really aggressive. So this guy now realizes he's in a world of shit and takes off for the door. Well, the big guy sidesteps, and the little guy runs right into him. Ooooof. Big mistake. He made first contact, so this huge dude delivers a righteous smackdown, and this little guy gets the courage knocked out of him.

And then everyone else pounces and drags him and practically throws him into his car. He flips us the bird and drives off. That was my first cancel. Since then, I've sworn to never be the guy who steps aside again.

I spoke to that big dude after the rally, and he said something I'll never forget. "If we are not escalating, we are retreating." I'll never forget that.

Todd could hardly believe that a national story was taking place in his hometown. He texted his mom and said he might need air mattresses from the garage and sleeping bags.

He asked the message board if there'd been a call to action yet and was told there'd been complete silence. Todd fell into his favorite spot on the couch in the living room and clicked between the cable news channels and read articles about Anne Prince on his phone. An hour passed, and he barely moved except when the sun glared off the television, and he got up to pull the curtains closed.

Tdooley: The thing is, nobody gives a shit. Some wacko religious nut is shaming women and spreading her anti-women poison, and the media isn't destroying her. And the police! What the hell are those pant loads of fail doing? A criminal breaks into a women's clinic, and all the fascists in blue say is, "Pass the popcorn?"

Sandybeaches: Idk.

Tdooley: We better get a text soon from leadership. Or I'm gone. I'm serious. I'm gone. This group hasn't done shit in three months."

Sandybeaches: IKR?

Tdooley: I'm not tied to this area. I'll bounce. F this. There's real activity going down at Berkley and San Fran. I mean, real platform denying get in their face shit, y' know.

Sandybeaches: Maybe something will come in today.

Fascisthunter9: Just got on. You guys hear anything?

Tdooley: Y' mean other than the sound of thumbs being inserted deeply into anal cavities?

Sandybeaches: IKR?

Fascisthunter9: I'm ready to go rouge.

Tdooley: Ha! You guys just wanna head out there? Just us? This shit needs to stop.

Sandybeaches: I think you meant "rogue."

Tdooley: Inside joke.

Sandybeaches: OK. Whatevs. I say, let's give them some time. They're probably just figuring their angle.

Fascisthunter9: Shit's only been going down since this morning.

Tdooley: BS. Started yesterday. Almost 24 hours ago. F this. I'm going if I don't hear something soon.

Wokeandbroke: Guys, I don't mean to be THAT GUY but this conversation really belongs on the "Take Action" message board. Not in the general message board. This is a local issue.

Tdooley: Local issue. WTF? Then why am I watching it on CNN, bitch?

Wokeandbroke: Regardless of the coverage, this is a local issue and should be on the "Take Action" board, not the general conversation board.

Tdooley: What are you talking about? Every event is local to somewhere shitforbrains. That doesn't mean every event is a local issue. If it's on ALL the cable news channels, it ceases to be merely a local news event, a-hole.

Wokeandbroke: The fact is you're calling for action so it should be on the "Take Action" board. Why is that so hard to understand?

Tdooley: Oh, I see so the general message board is just for people who want to theoretically talk about resisting fascism but not actually. So it's the pussy board?

Sandybeaches: I don't like that word.

Wokeandbroke: I'm just saying that I've been on this board for like eight months, and the way it works is you post something on the "take action" board, and if the moderator deems it worthy then they move it to the general board for everyone.

Tdooley: So ur telling me to post on a thread where nobody looks in the hope that some asleep-at-the-wheel moderator deems me worthy to bring into general thread? F that. All these fucking rules is exactly why nobody ever does anything.

Sandybeaches: I just don't understand why cowardly inaction is associated with a female body part, especially when most of the cowards are males.

Haymaker23: I'm a moderator on this board. I am not asleep at the wheel. In fact, I'm very aware of what's going on. No cowardice here.

Tdooley: Well, are you aware of what's going on in Thebes and how the fascists are protecting their own and the media is running pictures to make this criminal girl look sympathetic?

Haymaker23: There will be a text shortly. Keep your powder dry.

Bam42: Wtf? What powder?

Sandybeaches: It's like a civil war reference or some shit, meaning "chill."

Tdooley: We should be dragging her out!!! If we don't do something the fascists will make her a national hero. I'm warning you.

Wokeandbroke: Haymaker, wouldn't you agree that this thread should've originated on the "Take Action" board?

Tdooley: Holy crap, dude. Let it go. Obviously, he doesn't or else this thread would've been moved there.

Sandybeaches: ikr?

Todd descended the stairs and dressed in black. He constantly checked his phone for updates. He typed a message on his phone. :"This is just the largest effin story in the country right now. So yeah, it makes sense that the only group defending individual women's rights just stand on the sidelines, right?"

No response.

He sat on the edge of his bed watching the television news channels. "This bitch has got to pay!" he yelled to no one.

At 2:07 p.m. he received an alert from Haymaker.

Come out in force to disrupt the national spectacle!

In recent years, a few ultra-right-wing states have passed laws mandating that "a miscarried or aborted fetus must be interred or cremated." That legislation is being fought in the courts, but now an anti-abortion zealot in Thebes County, Pennsylvania, has upped the ante by stealing biological waste from a women's clinic and intends to hold a public funeral to shame women so that legislators can take away all reproductive rights from women in this country. Hello, Handmaid's Tale. Local police refuse to enter the church because the criminal is related to the district attorney.

This spectacle strikes at the heart of personhood discussions that need to take place in our country. The police's inaction lends support to the highly problematic assumption that fetuses must be treated as persons. This is a deadly serious attack on abortion rights because it seeks to impose the moral views of a fringe minority on us all.

The fascist cabal of the police, the media, and the Catholic Church are actively conspiring to protect this anti-abortionist zealot who broke into a women's clinic. Are local police not acting because they are under orders?

Join us to protest. Bring yourself, bring your friends, bring your crew, and come prepared to disrupt this nationally televised nightmare.

Yes! Todd thought.

RememberCharlottesville: I'm there!

 RoseCityReject: OMW!!!!!!!!!!!

 CableStreet13: Be there. Van full of goodies.

 Champingatthebit: Can anyone give me a ride?

 Cablestreet13: DM me.

 Doxxingandboxing01: Finally!

 Unapologeticallyinyourgrill: Two hours out. I've got three with me. Been watching the news all day. Ready!!!!

 JusticeNow99: Full tank of gas, enough weed to make a cancer ward dance, and a boner for violence. Let's do this.

 Whynotme: I'm there.

 Tdooley: Meet me there! The whole country's gonna' hear from us. #fightthefascists

On his way out the door, Todd pulled on a hooded sweatshirt and a trench coat. He also pulled his old red bike lock out of the closet and stuck it up his sleeve.

31

OFFICERS HARDAWAY AND DOUGHERTY looked out over the growing crowd in front of the church.

First, it had been a dozen white news vans with colorful logos on the sides and large satellite dishes on top crowded into the parking lot of the small Catholic parish. Journalists and camera crews mingled in the parking lot drinking coffee and staring at their phones while waiting for the next live shot or an update from the police.

Shortly after the first news reports aired, a number of politically progressive residents mixed with those Dougherty called "looky-loos" looking for a front-row seat to the spectacle, gathered behind the yellow tape the officers had run between two trees.

Dougherty spoke at length to a middle-aged bleached-blonde named Glynn who stood just behind the tape. Hardaway walked up and interrupted, smacking Dougherty on the arm with the back of his hand. He nodded toward a travel bus that came to a stop across the street. "More protesters," Hardaway said.

"These ones ain't like the looky-loos," Dougherty said as they filed out. "They're paid as sure as you and me.. They came by bus together. They've got professional signs, and they'll switch out every eight hours or so. You'll see."

Throughout the day, Dougherty pointed out to Glynn and Hardaway how the group mostly just stood around until the cameras turned on and then chanted and yelled for a few minutes before going back to checking their phones.

"Seems phony," Glynn said. "You good with that?"

"I like it when I understand why someone's doing something," Dougherty said, looking to Hardaway for agreement. "Like Glynn is obviously here because she can't get enough of me, right?"

She laughed and pushed him playfully.

"Listen, Hardaway," Dougherty said. "Would *you* be here if you weren't paid?"

"Nope," Hardaway replied. "I'd be fishing."

"Right, but it don't mean you don't believe in the law, right" Dougherty said. "Look, the reporters are all paid to be here. That don't mean they don't believe in freedom of the press. So, it just makes sense that the protesters are getting their cut. Welcome to America."

However, when the final wave of protesters arrived in the afternoon, Dougherty tensed and suggested to Glynn that perhaps it was best if she went home.

"Maybe they're just like the others," Glynn said while watching a group clad in black with masks over their faces climb out of a rusty van.

"No," Dougherty replied, "these folks are angry."

"At who?" Hardaway asked.

"At that girl for breaking into a women's clinic. At the church for harboring a wanted criminal. They're angry at us for not dragging her out. Mostly, they're angry at the world for not being as angry as them."

"You got all that from them getting out a van?" Glynn asked, back and forth between the group and Dougherty.

"The devil is in the details," Dougherty said. "And there's lots of details here."

Hardaway gave him a look. "You saying these folks are the devil?"

"I'm not sure I believe the devil is real," Dougherty said, "but if he is, I'm betting he's close by about now."

Dougherty repeated his recommendation for Glynn to head home. He lifted the police tape, and she ducked under it. He watched her get into her yellow Mercedes parked across the street.

"You actually seem scared," Hardaway said, teasing the older officer.

Dougherty raised his eyebrows. "Me? I'm not smart enough to be scared, but you should be."

Comments from *Thebes Weekly News* website:

1. Doesn't anyone see this ending badly? Violence. Their death is the doing of their own conscious hand.

2. Shelter from the cold and rain, we escaped the terrible plagues, and now man can send his thoughts all across the globe quicker than the wind to civilizations ruled by law. We have tamed the earth and bent

creation to our will. But we haven't conquered ourselves. And in the end, from Death alone we will find no rescue. Why doesn't she give herself up?

3. Wait, the Catholic Church is harboring criminals? Who could've seen this coming?

4. Like father like daughter, passionate, wild . . . she hasn't learned to bend before adversity.

32

Michael Olden had arrived at St. Stephen the Martyr Parish along with the morning Mass regulars. That morning, however, they were turned away by police at the steps of the church, so Michael asked each parishioner if they would pray the rosary with him right there.

"If you're leaving, please do so now," Hardaway said. "If you're staying you'll need to get behind the yellow tape with the others."

In the end, Michael, along with four other elderly parishioners, including an eighty-five-year-old great-grandmother who stood all of four feet ten inches, took a spot just behind the police line and prayed the rosary. The first decade went on without any interruption, but soon a group of young protesters from a local college wearing do-rags over their mouths crowded the four, chanting, "Get your rosaries off my ovaries." But the tiny group persisted until the end even when they could no longer hear themselves.

When Michael arrived home, he called the local pro-life group, PA 4 Life, an organization he'd donated to yearly. After being placed on hold several times, a woman named Stacy introduced herself as the outreach coordinator.

"Hi, my name is Michael Olden. I don't know if you've been made aware—".

"Excuse me sir, excuse me. I'm gonna' stop you right there," Stacy said. "Sir, we are *very* aware of what's going on in Thebes County right now."

"Ohhhkay?" Michael replied, leaning on his kitchen table unsure why she was speaking to him like he was a bratty three-year-old. "But the reason I'm calling is this seems to be a good opportunity to stand with a fellow pro-lifer. There are, right now, hundreds of pro-abortion protesters outside our parish, and I thought—"

"Sir, sir. Sir, I appreciate your past support, but I want to be clear. I don't know you or what your perspective is—"

"I'm Michael Olden. I . . .I . . ."

"Sir," she said as if praying for patience, "we in the pro-life community have worked for many years to ensure people view the pro-life community as peaceful, helpful, and non-confrontational. We have sought to change hearts and minds in a charged and politicized environment. The media, as you know, is not very friendly toward us. And now with one action, this Anne Prince has set the pro-life movement back decades by giving the pro-choice community all the ammunition it needs to demonize us. We will not stand with this person. In fact, we issued a press release this morning denouncing her."

"Oh," Michael said, sitting at his kitchen table.

"Furthermore," Stacy continued, "I would ask you to discourage any local pro-lifers from publicly supporting her. Listen, Mr. Oldman, I know you think you're doing good, but sometimes local pro-lifers, though well intentioned, don't have the proper perspective, especially on issues that are of a more . . . national scale."

"I'm not sure I understand," Michael said.

"Thank you for the call, sir," she said with finality. "God bless."

It took Michael a few seconds to realize she'd hung up. "Oh," he said to no one. He walked out of his kitchen, pushed the phone into his pocket, and sat in his chair. He found himself bouncing his knee and twisting his lips, and it took him a moment to accept that he was angry. Yup, absolutely pissed.

Michael looked at his wife's empty chair. "Can you believe the way she spoke to me?"

Silence.

Michael breathed loudly and prayed. When he finished he looked at his wife's chair again. "That poor young girl is being abandoned."

He stood and pulled his "Abortion stops a beating heart" sign from the closet and walked out the door.

He returned to the church alone that morning amid about 200 protest-ers calling for the immediate arrest (or worse) of Anne Prince. The cameras all found him immediately, and the reporters peppered him with questions.

"Do you know Anne Prince personally?"

"Um, she seems like a sweet girl. I've never had the pleasure of con-versing with her at any length, but I've seen her at Mass. I noticed her be-cause it's rare to see young people attend daily Mass. In fact, I think I'm one of the youngest of our little group. If you want to feel young, attend daily Mass." He laughed.

"Why are you supporting a criminal?"

"I believe some distinction needs to be made between the activity and the person," Michael said. "I do share her belief that every life is sacred. I also believe God loves everyone, and if I can just remind her of that one little fact in the worst moment of her life, my time will have been well spent, don't you think?

"Do you believe the child is her father's?"

"Excuse me?" Michael said, puzzled.

"Should abortion be illegal even in cases of rape or incest?"

"I believe God loves everyone. Everyone," Michael said. "No matter who they are or what they've done."

"What would you say to the millions of women who are offended by Anne Prince's actions?"

"I pray every Wednesday and Sunday outside the abortion clinic, so what Anne did is not something I would do, but she has been through a difficult time in . . . um . . . recent days with the death of her father, and she is deserving of . . ." The noise grew, and he had to yell to be heard. He paused before continuing. "I do, however, believe it's ironic that none of these people protested the clinic tossing unborn children into dumpsters, but they're outraged now that Anne Prince is attempting to honor the victims of abortion."

Suddenly, Michael felt hands and arms pushing him from behind. One man just behind him in a black baseball cap and dark sunglasses yelled to the cameras over and over, "Don't normalize the Nazi!" Others surged forward, pushing the old man into the yellow tape. One cameraman retreated as Michael tried desperately to maintain his balance but finally fell over the tape and rolled into the feet of a cameraman. The crowd cheered. "I've fallen and I can't get up!" one man yelled as Michael attempted to untangle his feet from the yellow tape. A ripple of laughter ran through the protestors.

Officer Hardaway helped Michael to his feet as a reporter on a live feed summed up the situation. "As you can see, both sides of this contentious debate in Thebes County are impassioned, and I fear what might happen if this issue is not resolved."

When Michael regained his footing and took his place again behind the tape, he noticed his sign had been taken. He turned around and saw it being passed overhead deep into the crowd. Gone. Michael looked at Hardaway, who shrugged. "Maybe it's time to go home, old-timer." Michael thanked him and continued praying his rosary alone.

Within two hours, a handful of parishioners joined Michael, saying they'd seen him on television and been inspired. An hour later, about twenty pro-lifers were crowding around Michael. One tall young blond man who looked like he had just walked off the beach stood next to Michael and yelled to the crowd. "Everyone! My name is Jason, and these nice Christian pro-lifers might not believe in violence, but I'm your worst nightmare. I'm a pro-life atheist, and if just one of you asshats touches this old man again, this Marine will tear through all y'all like only a Marine can." This afforded a little more space to the pro-lifers, some of whom held homemade signs that said "Life is Sacred," "Honor the Dead," and "We support Anne Prince."

Soon after, a few dozen pro-lifers stood with Michael with signs expressing their support of Anne or life in general. The number of pro-choice protesters grew exponentially. Many who arrived around dusk wore masks and goggles. Michael took little notice of them and spoke at length with Jason throughout the day and prayed.

By late afternoon, about six Christians associated with a local Baptist church arrived arm in arm and joined Michael in prayer—a low murmur under the protesters' chants. In frustration, one woman began yelling her prayer, but Michael reached out to her. "It only has to be loud enough for God to hear," he said.

33

DAMAGE CONTROL. *THINK,* ALLIE told herself. *Map it out.*

She sat at her desk, head in her hands. *Figure it out,* she urged herself. *Think it through.*

OK. Some in the media probably already knew there was a video showing her dumping biological materials in the dumpster. The phone rang incessantly to discuss the Anne Prince situation, but she hadn't yet offered comment outside of the press release. Yet.

Some of the journalists mentioned the video in their questions, and she feared that soon it would become part of the story if she didn't get out in front of it.

The video had two ramifications. 1) Legalities. She could face charges for Illegal dumping of medical waste if she did nothing to a) have the videos removed b) discredit them. If she didn't do a) or b), she would face at least a fine. She had acted as the director of the clinic, so the clinic would pay. She would, however, be fired. Broke and fired with two daughters. That was where she stood. Two daughters who would have to be removed from their private school. Two daughters who looked to her to solve their problems. She could already see their crying faces when they learned they'd be leaving all their friends . . .

Stop! Focus!

2) Public relations. A total disaster. The clinic would be exposed to a world of damaging media, and she would lose her career or at least be transferred to Philadelphia in disgrace.

The entire situation would be scrutinized because of the heightened press awareness of the standoff at the church. Yes, Allie had done this to herself, first by dumping the waste and second by sending out the press release. But she couldn't look back. Forward. Only forward.

It all seemed so jumbled in her mind. Until it hit her. A two-pronged attack. The video needed to be discredited and Anne Prince blamed. The girl had to be totally discredited, so anything she said about the clinic dumping materials wouldn't be believed.

The press would believe anything about Anne at this point, but Allie couldn't talk to the media because too many direct questions would be asked. Anne, however, also couldn't speak to the media, at least until she came out of the church, so Allie could frame the narrative if she acted first. But it couldn't come from her. No. It had to be from someone else. She thought of Rachel, but she didn't want corporate to have any knowledge of this.

She knew what she had to do. She called Denice into her office.

34

ANNE PRINCE HAD INSTANTLY become the greatest enemy of reproductive choice. Denice understood the danger she posed. Yes, Anne remained stuck inside the church for now but could emerge as the perfect avatar for the patriarchy, a rallying point for anti-abortion zealots, a young, attractive woman eager to turn the clock back on women.

Anne could expose the clinic for disposing of products of conception in the dumpster. The fetus fetishists would latch onto this and make a hero of her, reigniting a national debate over women's rights, acting as the thin edge of the wedge in this dangerous time. It was up to Denice to stop her.

Allie folded her hands in front of her while seated at her desk and explained to Denice why she had disposed of the medical waste, the reaction corporate would have, how Anne Prince had to take the blame for this, and how she could—

"OK," Denice interrupted. "Just tell me what you need me to do."

The speed with which Denice accepted the plan shocked Allie. When Allie finished laying it out, Denice laughed. "OK," she said, " you get the video taken down, and I'll do everything else."

Allie wondered again if Denice was giving her attitude, which Denice mistook for newfound respect.

Denice believed the older generation failed to understand young people. In the 1960s and 1970s, women were on fire demanding equal rights, and great gains were made, but in the ensuing decades, women lost their momentum. No longer revolutionaries, they settled in to acting as stewards. This young generation, however, sought to advance women's rights and would stop at nothing to advance the cause.

Denice walked past the church and the graveyard, not nervous but anxious. She'd waited her entire life to champion women's rights on the biggest stage. "That's so Denice," everyone would say.

As she walked alongside the police tape, a voice called out a hello, and she saw the old man who prayed in front of the clinic smiling at her and raising his hand to wave. Ech. She looked away.

As she walked past the church window, she thought of Anne Prince isolated inside. She wished she could speak with her and explain why her thinking was tragically outdated and harmful to women. But Anne had chosen a side. She had chosen to stand alone against the laws of our government and stand against the culture. She had to be resisted. Crushed.

She walked to the far side of the parking lot where the media congregated and approached a blond woman with a "Karen" haircut and a severe jawline leaning against the hood of a van and speaking to a group of reporters. A thrill ran through Denice because she recognized the woman from television. Denice stood outside their little circle, which didn't acknowledge her right away. She waited. A moment. Awkward. They were all aware of her presence but had no intention of talking to her or including her. Her anger rose, and she inspected them closely, critically. The blonde with the Karen haircut had terrible acne, which she concealed with makeup. The ridiculously thin man with the serious blue jacket appeared sickly in person. And she thought the older journalist might have hair plugs. To Denice, they all seemed like old people trying to maintain their hold on power.

Finally, she decided to announce herself. "My name is Denice Williams. I'm an associate at the Elizabeth Blackwell Clinic, and I was assaulted by Anne Prince."

"Jawline" stood erect, blue eyes wide. "Hair Plugs" peeled his torso from the hood of the car. Denice had their attention.

"Hold on. Hold on. We've got to get set up here." The reporters scattered. Denice expected a scramble. She expected elation. Instead they pulled on their jackets, fixed their hair, screwed in their earpieces, and readied their cameras. Nobody spoke to her.

Jawline sidled up next to Denice. "Am I in the shot?" she asked. Her cameraman nodded. Nobody even looked at Denice until they were all set. Jawline adopted a look of extreme sympathy. "Please share your story," he said.

Lights on. Microphones under her chin.

"I just wanted to let everyone know I'm a victim," she said. "Anne Prince assaulted me."

"Whoa, whoa, whoa!" one cameraman yelled.

"Holy crap. Who are you?" another said.

"How about a name? Jeez!" another voice said. "Let's do this again."

"Oh, I'm sorry," Denice said, embarrassed. "My name is Denice Williams. I'm a supervisor with the Elizabeth Blackwell Clinic for Women. I didn't want to say this before, but when Anne Prince entered the clinic, she pushed me. Assaulted me. I didn't mention this to police earlier because I was so focused on how this crime affected the clinic and attempted to shame women. But I believe this rises to the level of a hate crime and should be prosecuted as such."

A dozen microphones and about eight cameras surrounded her. She counted. Dozens of journalists stood on the periphery writing notes.

"Because of patient confidentiality, I can't say if Anne Prince was a client at the Blackwell Clinic and was perhaps later made to feel guilty about some choices she made because of her fundamentalist strain of religion, but I'm saying we've seen her at the clinic before. Let's just say that. It's quite possible this is also not the first time she has stolen biological materials from the clinic. We're not saying for sure, but we are investigating the possibility that some products of conception are missing, and it is possible anti-abortion activists have stolen biological materials from the women's clinic as part of a desperate attempt to shame women and their choices.

"Initial findings of our investigation indicate that someone may have entered previously and stolen medical waste and placed it in dumpsters in an attempt to make the clinic look bad. YouTube has already blocked one user, an anti-abortion radical, for posting a highly edited, thoroughly debunked video that has subsequently been removed from YouTube.

"Clinics all around the country have seen stunts like this with doctored videos created by anti-women zealots in an attempt to shame women and play politics and limit their reproductive choices. In recent weeks, we have seen anti-abortionists in our dumpsters several times and chased them away, though we didn't call the police. Anne Prince may well have been involved in these attempts."

"The Blackwell Clinic hopes for a peaceful resolution to this ugly and politically charged situation and urges the police and the district attorney to end this standoff sooner rather than later. The Blackwell Clinic also hopes charges will be pressed and violators sentenced to the fullest extent of the law, regardless of who this terrorist—yes, I said it—regardless of who this anti-abortion terrorist is related to. Justice should be blind when it comes to women's rights—and all rights for that matter. Thank you."

She had improvised the terrorist bit, but she believed Anne Prince was a terrorist who would harm women if given the chance.

Allie had instructed her not to answer questions, just thank them and walk away, then return to the clinic. And she did.

By the time Denice arrived, Allie was sitting at her desk hunched over her monitor watching the news on her computer. Denice walked in without knocking and came around the far side of the desk. She saw herself on the screen and gasped. It looked like she had a double chin. *What a terrible angle,* she thought.

When Allie looked up from the screen, Denice saw she'd been crying, her mouth twisted and mascara clotting on her lashes.

"What's wrong?" Denice asked. "The plan worked, right?"

"Yes, it worked," Allie said. "You did exactly what I asked, but I never should've asked you to do that. How could I have been so stupid? I can't believe I risked everything. My husband . . . my daughters . . . just so stupid. I risked everything for . . . for nothing. Thank you, Denice, thank you. I don't know what I would've done without you. I . . . never should've asked you to do that. It wasn't right."

Denice reached out and touched Allie's shoulder, a gesture that would've been unimaginable for her just a few hours earlier. "Allie, you did what's best for the clinic every step of the way. You protected the clinic. Nobody can fault you for that. What's good for the clinic is what's good for women. You're brilliant. Implying Anne had been a client here without saying it makes the anti-abortionists hate her, and we already hate her because she poses a danger to women. I mean, she's got, like, nobody on her side now. Brilliant. I'm like personally so grateful to have you as a role model."

Allie looked up at her. Denice blushed and thought about her chin.

Together, they watched a news report that said Anne may have been a client at the Blackwell clinic, which initiated an investigation to uncover a plot by anti-abortionists to steal biological materials in an attempt to embarrass the clinic.

The news showed a picture of Anne from her high school yearbook. Allie thought she looked like someone her daughters might know. The reporter, standing in front of the crowd at the church, said Anne could be facing even more serious charges and jail time.

Allie looked away. "My God, what have I done?"

Comments on the CNN website:

1. These disingenuous, outlandish tactics used by anti-abortion advocates have led to violence for decades, but the idea of fetal personhood, which is what this is really about, is one of the most insidious and dangerous developments. Every woman and every American should be very concerned. The attempt to give embryos and fetuses rights superseding the rights of women would make abortion a felony.

2. This stunt is a backdoor attempt to increase the ability of right-wing politicians to police the bodies of pregnant people.

3. For decades, harassment, stalking, and death threats to workers at women's clinics have been a part of regular life. But this year it's been worse than ever. And this is an example of it. Providers have seen an uptick in violence this year, against themselves and their clinics. Many say these often go unreported because violence is so commonplace.

4. The Very Reverend Elizabeth Watson-Torres, an Episcopal priest and chief executive officer of Women Against Violence, said in an interview that just aired that violence that providers face today is "beyond anything we've ever seen before."

5. This latest crime by an anti-abortion activist is an egregious "in your face" attempt to devalue the agency of women.

6. This is violence against women!

35

MILTON PUSHED THROUGH THE heavy oak door of his office into the wide, empty, grey stone hallway. For many years he had gotten a thrill from working there. Many mornings he still felt a tiny thrill as he drove up to the thick stone pillars and the clock on the high tower. It was the center of something. And he was the rock through the window. The middle finger.

Everything had always been so clear there. He was there defending one person against the system. He acted as their champion. Hell, he *was* their champion. For some, he would be the only person who ever took their side against the crushing wheel of the state. Yeah, sometimes it was just a DUI or an assault, and sometimes it was someone who needed drug counseling and not prison, but it was him standing up for the little guy against city hall.

But now he wasn't the middle finger. He was the fist.

His footfalls echoed in the hallway. He saw Tyrese cleaning out a coffee pot behind his counter and quickened his pace.

"How are you today, Mr. Milton?" Tyrese called out.

Milton stopped as if caught and smiled. "The Amazing Tyrese. You know, I'm working on a theory that says maybe you're not really blind after all. How did you know it was me?"

"When the good Lord takes one sense away, he gives another," Tyrese said. "You heading to your brother's house to console your grieving family?"

"You should set up a fortune-telling stand," Milton said. "You'd probably make more on that than you do on coffee."

"I don't know. People like their coffee."

Milton stood there, the silence elongating into awkwardness. "I am actually going to see Anne. What do you think of that?"

"Oh, you bear your burdens, and I'll bear mine. It's better that way; believe me. You don't wanna hear what I have to say."

"You're right. I probably don't," Milton said. He took a few steps and then stopped. Waited.

"Mr. Milton, there was a wonderful little town in India back in the day. Just about perfect. But they had one little problem, y' unnastand. Cobras. Not a lot, but one had to be careful. Now, this is around the time the British took charge. They loved the town too and thought they could make it perfect. So, they offered a bounty for each dead cobra someone turned in. Smart, right? So, people went out and killed just about every cobra they saw. But some enterprising types began breeding cobras in order to get the money. Well, the British didn't take over the world by being stupid, so they caught on to the scam and canceled the program. Since the snakes no longer had any value, the cobra breeders just released them out into the wild. Now, there were cobras everywhere biting people, y' unnastand, and just about everyone up and left the town."

"I'm sorry I asked," Milton said, turning once again to leave.

"Sir, I fear for you," Tyrese said. "I fear you'll lose not only your entire family today but possibly yourself."

"Come on, Tyrese, I think you're overblowing this," he said. "In a week the media and all the attention will be elsewhere, and this will be forgotten."

"The good Lord ain't indifferent to what's going on here today."

"I'm under immense pressure here," Milton said, lowering his voice and approaching the counter. "It's about playing it smart."

"Mr. Milton, the British were smart, but the cobras still won."

"What in hell am I supposed to do? You think I should just let Anne go? How can I look the people of this county in the eye after that? I can't look at this in a vacuum. You have to see the bigger picture."

"You're sitting on the razor's edge," Tyrese said.

"I'm trying to save my niece. I'm the only lifeline she has here."

"No, Mr. Milton, I believe she's *your* only lifeline."

36

SHADOWS DANCED ON THE stone walls of the church. Anne knelt in the front row, staring at the crucifix above the altar.

Outside, the crowd noise exploded. Rumbling, roars, grunts, and exhalations intensified and reverberated through the walls. Anne looked up from her prayers toward the stained glass.

Paul, still crouched in the balcony, considered approaching her, but then the front doors of the church opened. He couldn't see the doors from his vantage point, but saw a dark shadow stretched over the nave of the church.

The police? A protester?

"Hello, Anne," a figure said, allowing the door to close behind him. Anne rose from her kneeling position to stand at the foot of the sanctuary. She walked steadily down the center aisle toward the approaching figure.

"Am I speaking to Uncle Milton or to the district attorney?" she queried into the darkness.

He wore a blue suit and polished shoes. "Can't I be both?" he asked with forced joviality.

"No," Anne said. She reached him halfway down the aisle and hugged him. He kissed her cheek. "If you're here as the district attorney, you're not here as my uncle. I've known politics well enough to know that. Give me some credit."

"Credit?" he scoffed. "You want credit for this?" He gestured toward the crowd outside.

"Have you eaten?" Anne asked. "You look drained."

"I can't imagine why," he said, sitting in a pew. "The last week has been so uneventful."

She smiled and sat in the row in front of him. He leaned forward, his tone personal. "Anne, this has gotten way out of hand. Hundreds of people are outside calling for you to be locked up—or worse. The national media is vilifying you, let me tell you. People are looking to me—"

"I'm sorry this affected you," she said.

"Oh, don't worry about me," he said. "Other people are paid to do that now. No use doing it for free."

She smiled, and he leaned back in the pew with his arm stretched atop the backrest. She noticed the shirt under his suit jacket and tie was wrinkled.

Anne asked about Susan Doyle's condition and said the media hadn't reported on her. "Susan will recover," he said. "I'm told she has an infection, and the doctors are dealing with it. She'll be fine."

"Told? You didn't go see her?" Anne asked, a little shocked.

"I've been a little busy," he said sharply.

Once again, silence grew between them.

"Anne," Milton said finally, "if you don't mind me asking, what's the objective here?"

Anne turned to face him. "Uncle Milton, they were throwing the bodies of babies into dumpsters. I couldn't stand the thought that my brother, your nephew, would be discarded like trash. I intend to honor our dead. I will pray for him."

"Kiddo, there are ways to go about this," he said. "There are laws against illegal dumping of biohazardous waste, and there could've been prosecutions. But now you've muddled that, and the media is saying those videos were doctored . . ."

Anne smiled bitterly and turned away.

"What?" Milton asked, knowing he'd upset her. "I clearly said something you don't like, but for the life of me—"

"I just told you that your nephew's life was taken, and he may have been discarded in a dumpster, and you cited a misdemeanor offense about illegal dumping and told me about the media," she said. "There's no doubt who entered this church tonight. And it is not my uncle."

"Come on, Anne. Give me a break," he said. "This is ridiculous."

Milton stood and walked out into the middle aisle .. "You've broken the law, Anne. There's no way around that." He spoke with increasing speed and volume. His intense tone and his hand chopping the air in front of him made it easy to picture him in court just like that, delivering closing arguments. "You will be charged. You know that too, right? This has gone far beyond a local crime story. The national media is calling for your head. You should read the emails my office is receiving from all over the country. Did you think that because of who your father was or because I'm the district attorney you could avoid responsibility? If you think that, you're wrong. In fact, because of who you are, you have a higher responsibility."

"On that we agree," she said flatly, facing forward again. "I do have a higher responsibility."

"Ah, I assume you're talking about your God," he said, raising his eyes toward the ceiling. "Well, God will not shield you from consequences either. Did you think he would save you from all this?"

"No. I believed something like this might happen," she said. "I don't welcome the consequences, but I accept them. And perhaps God can bring some good out of this evil."

"I see. So everyone but you is evil in this little drama you've created. Everyone but you." His tone was mocking now.

She turned toward him. "Please don't do that to me. I haven't said anything like that. Please don't make this a thing about me being judgmental or holier than thou. I'm simply trying to do right by my unborn brother."

"I see, it's all about your . . . principles," he continued in the same mocking tone, "and damn the consequences to everyone else—including your family?" he added as if he'd checkmated her.

"It's because I care that I couldn't allow our family to be discarded anymore, Mr. District Attorney." She stood and hurled each enunciated syllable of his title at him. "My father discarded us. He tore this family apart in every possible way. Had he simply died, our family would've mourned but remained intact. But doing . . . what he did, he not only took our father from us, he took away every moment, every memory we ever had of him. My father tossed away his family like trash. I will not allow it to happen again."

Milton looked away. He paced back a few rows in silence and then stopped. "Your father loved you."

Silence.

"He did," he insisted.

"I know that," she said. "But if love doesn't dictate action, what is it?"

Milton paced again while Anne sat and returned her eyes to the golden tabernacle in the front of the church. He followed her eyeline and looked around slowly, taking in the candles, the stained glass, the crucifix. "It's been a while since I've been here."

"See? I told you God can bring good out of even the worst situations," she said, smiling.

He shook his head and chuckled. "Always the optimist."

"All Christians must be optimists at heart," she said playfully. "We have no choice. Even the worst moments are opportunities of grace."

"Is that what Christians thought when they were being fed to lions?"

"I believe so, yes."

He looked at her affectionately. "You're so much like your father," he said and saw her eyes burn at the comment. He held his hands up in playful surrender. "Oh no, no, I mean that in the nicest way possible. You've always had a way of attacking with your eyes. I've witnessed their silent scorn a hundred times. You've had that in your personal arsenal ever since you were the tiniest creature. I've always found that so . . . impressive about you. There never existed an injustice small enough to be ignored by you, no miniscule wrong that wouldn't spark your ire. No principle too small for a standoff. That's your father in you. He had the perfect life, but happiness didn't interest him. I'll admit it made him perfect for his job as prosecutor. Any and every perceived injustice instantly became the focal point of his existence until corrected. But Anne, the world is unbalanced, and so are people. You have to accept it. You have to learn to . . . tilt your head just so until everything looks fine again. Your father obsessed over justice, as you know. And sometimes, oftentimes, his family paid the price. I know you felt that. But I'll admit I've never shared his obsession. It's taken me some time, but I've realized I'm not my brother. I believe every situation must be looked at through a prism of pros and cons that must be weighed and not held to some impossible standard. Each situation must be judged on its own. Context is crucial."

Anne nodded. "I agree, but I also think you can contextualize anything into meaninglessness. In the end, there is right and there is wrong. Shouldn't you, as district attorney, be most concerned with that?"

"Back to me, huh? It's interesting how the whole world is focused on you right now, but somehow you want to make this about me."

She shrugged. "I'm worried about you."

"Me? Y' know, Anne, I didn't search out this job. I didn't need it. It filled no great hole in my life. I was happily running my law practice defending the poor, the needy, and minorities, those most often oppressed by people like your father. And then, just as I doubted my path, they offered me this job. Now this is my job. This is not about my private feelings. This is about me wanting to help the greatest number of people. Isn't that what you say your religion is all about, helping people? I would think you'd be sympathetic. This job allows me to help greater numbers. That's why I took it and why I'm committed to that path."

"I know you are," Anne said, looking at him with a sort of sad affection. "I don't doubt your commitment, Uncle Milton. I just worry what you've committed to. I said my 'yes' to God. You said 'yes' to what?"

"Don't try to antagonize me. It's like you're trying to . . ." He paused as he searched for an answer. Then his eyes lit up, and he wagged his finger at her. "It's like you're trying to get me to throw the book at you. Is that what you want? To be a martyr? No. No. Anne, you're a young girl grieving her father. I understand that. All you have to do is apologize, and I'll get you parole or perhaps even just mandatory counseling. Just come outside with me now and end it. How's that sound?"

She shook her head, resolute. "I will never apologize for honoring my brother."

"Listen, if you attempt to hold a funeral or try to bury the . . . biological remains, this will get out of control, and there will be . . ." He stopped himself and attempted to reduce it to one simple fact. He held his hands out in front of him as if explaining something simple to a child. "Anne, you're breaking the law."

"Man's law maybe. But I'm honoring God's law."

"Anne, come on!" Exasperated, he spun away. "I mean, come on now. Do you really believe in all this stuff?" He waved his hand around to indicate the church, the statues, and the tabernacle. "Do you believe that little fat priest—"

"Father Quinn?"

"OK. Do you believe Father Quinn has some abracadabra powers? Come on, Anne, you're too smart for that. You believe a silly man has magical powers or that a ritual of piling a little dirt on a body means something? Or some words said by a fat man actually changes bread into something else?"

"I believe everything we do means more than we can ever understand."

"No. No. Don't be evasive and judgmental about what I'm saying," he chided. "Isn't that a sin? 'Judge not, lest ye be judged'?"

"I haven't judged anyone. I have merely said things I believe to be true. A human being died—my brother—and I plan to honor him."

"And this will right some wrong? This will get revenge upon your father's lover? Upon society?"

"Uncle, this child, your nephew, was disrespected in every way possible, declared unhuman," she said, her voice rising in pitch. "That is a horror. Every human being is worthy of respect. I will show to him in death what he was refused in life. That's all I have left to give. I don't care what happens after."

"That child's mother made a choice. Don't you believe in a woman's right to choose?"

"What about the child's choice?" she said in an urgent tone, her eyes alight. "And, to be clear, I've not said a word about Susan Doyle or choice. This is not about politics for me. How does me honoring the child she created with my father have anything to do with her choice? My heart breaks for her. I wish I'd run out of my father's funeral to console her because she needed someone, and I failed her. If I'd done right by her, my brother might still be alive. But I didn't, and I'm sorry for that. She discarded her child, and I'm sure she's hurting over that. I'm sick that I can't go to her and comfort her even though what she did hurt us all. And on top of everything that happened, the clinic tossed his remains into a dumpster. A dumpster! I'm offering some semblance of honor, dignity to the dead. I'm affording respect to those whom others discarded, but I'm the one surrounded by police?"

Milton laughed derisively and leaned forward with his head in his hands.

"Did I say something funny?" Anne asked.

"No, not at all. It just occurred to me. You want the consequences of this. My temperance, my contextualization in this matter doesn't frighten you. It offends you," he said as if he'd unlocked the key to everything. "My affection for you is an obstacle to what you actually want."

Anne shook her head. "I don't know what you're talking about."

"Oh, no, no, no. I've known you too long to believe that. Your mind works far too well not to have seen exactly where this is going. I know that despite all your simplistic pieties, it's still there, that searing intelligence. I must admit I'm surprised this faith thing of yours has lasted. It didn't surprise me you jumped into it. That's predictable, although I would've anticipated something a little more exotic like Buddhism or maybe some mysticism with crystals. But you were looking for answers, and there's a church on every street corner claiming to have it. We've all done it. We've all gone down that road. But most of us burn through it. We grow up. We accept reality for what it is, not a fairy tale. Look at this faith of yours. What has it brought the world but racism, misogyny, wars, and persecution? People have been performing the greatest acts of evil in the name of God since . . ." He searched for the right words in the air in front of him.

"Cain killed Abel?" she suggested. He smirked. "I would suggest," she said, "we would call those pre-existing conditions. We call it original sin."

"I know that's what Christians say." He walked toward the altar and turned. "Why, Anne? Why did you do this? You didn't even run from the clinic. You walked. It seems to me you wanted to get caught. You knew what would happen."

She shrugged. "I saw this as a possibility .."

"And what? Consequences be damned? You must do what you think is right regardless of who it affects?"

"Is that so hard to understand?"

"Yes!" he bellowed, his voice echoing throughout the sanctuary. "The scariest thing to some people is to be of no consequence. Is that it? You grew up being told, 'You're special. You're so smart. You're so good.' Or you've had this belief that Almighty God has a plan just for you. A big plan. But you get a little older, and guess what happens? You just get a little older. Until it dawns on you that maybe, just maybe, you're not that special. Maybe no plan ever existed. It's all just you flailing about, trying desperately to change the world. But guess what? The world doesn't want changing, and you can't do it anyway. And maybe that's what scares you. To not be able to move the levers of the world is one of the most frustrating experiences every young person has to go through. And it's a burning humiliation to understand you can't affect anything. I reach out. I touch, but nothing moves, as if I'm a ghost that people don't see or perhaps even pity.

"Look at me, I'm a district attorney not because of something I did. I've done good my whole life, worked hard. Helped people. But that didn't matter. I'm DA because my brother died, and I had the same last name. That's it. Pure chance. But what I do with this matters. Not to some bearded benevolent entity in the sky. It matters to me. It matters to actual people. I can now affect my world in greater ways, and I will. But I've got to give it to you. With one little action you've upset the entire town. And congratulations, you've become a spectacle for the entire country. You beat us all. Perhaps this was your wish all along. You've set something in motion bigger than yourself. And now we're all just puppets on your string doing what you knew we would do. But I won't, Anne. I'm not going to do it. You want me to make you into a martyr? I won't do it. I won't. For this to work, for all this to work, this must end with your persecution. That's been your goal all along. Poor Anne the martyr. But I'm not your puppet."

"I have no goal other than honoring my brother and recognizing that every life is sacred," Anne replied. "As hard as it may be for you to understand, there is no master plan. No manipulation."

"Ah, there's the insult. I'm the politician, so I must be manipulative and conniving, right?"

Anne shook her head. "I didn't say that.".

"Well, what would you have me do, Anne? No, seriously. Pretend you're me. You're the DA. Would you have me just turn my back on this?"

"I would hope you would do what you believe is right," she said. "And I ask no different."

"The people outside are incensed," he said. "You know you've stirred up a hornet's nest. You're not stupid. You've jumped into the middle of the most heated debate in our country right now. And you ran to a church of all places. This is the heart of it all, kiddo. The bloody center of this silent war tearing our country apart. Young vs. old. Progressive vs. conservative. Faith vs. science. Anti-abortion vs. choice. Honey, you're on the wrong side of history on this. You will lose."

"I'm not called to win," she said. "I'm called to fidelity. I just want to honor that which the world discarded. Why does the world care what I do? They've already declared the contents of a woman's womb meaningless, so why does it matter if I see meaning in the meaninglessness?"

"Everything must come to a point with you," he said throwing his hands up. "There are no rounded edges in your world. Bright lines and right angles, right?"

"I believe in right and wrong."

"The naïve view of youth. Everything is binary. Black and white. No gray at all, right?" He took a deep breath. "You know, Anne, I'm not unsympathetic to your views. I may even share some of them on a practical basis. But because of my position, I have to take a larger perspective. To be practical. If I let this issue define me, define my party, we will be run out of this county. We won't get elected dog catcher. And how do you think the other party will treat you and your views? It will be so much worse. So, if I come down hard on this, on you, it's because I care about people.

"Look, Anne, if I lose in the special election, the power goes to the other side, and they will close all your precious pro-life crisis pregnancy clinics. They will make it illegal for you to even come near a clinic after this.

They want to shut you up. And you're making that more likely. Do you understand that? You're the creator of your own worst nightmare. Be reasonable. If you care about the unborn like you say you do, walk outside with me now. End it. Walk out with me now, and things won't get worse. The status quo will continue." She looked at him compassionately as he continued, his words coming faster. "The pro-life community is not supporting you at all. Here," he said pulling out his phone. "I can read you a press release from the pro-life federation or something or other. They say you're hurting the cause. Don't you think these people know their cause and understand it, or do you always know better?"

Anne remained silent.

"Never mind that this is killing your family. Your sister is beside herself, sick with worry. She hasn't even told your mother what's going on yet. She won't let her watch television or listen to the radio. And . . ." He stopped talking, seeing her eyes weren't even on him anymore. "Anne, come outside with me right now. Please end this before it gets worse. I'll take you out myself. I have to give a press conference right now. If you surrender, that'll be the news. All the news vans will leave, and this will be forgotten. If you don't, it will get much worse for you, and I'll be forced to prosecute you to the fullest extent of the law."

Anne looked at him with concern, which he didn't appreciate. "That means prison, Anne! Prison!" he yelled, walking past her and approaching the door.

Just before leaving he lowered his head, his hand against the door. "Anne, please don't make me do this."

"I'm not making you do anything," she said, her eyes softening. "I love you, Uncle Milton, but just as I must decide what I must do, so must you."

She knelt in the pew and turned toward the tabernacle. "Uncle Milton, I'm here to pray for the dead. Stay with me. Father Quinn will be here, and we can pray for my brother, your nephew. We can pray for my father's soul. We can also pray for Izzy, my mom, and for Susan Doyle, who I'm sure is devastated and hurting. We can pray for you. Stay here and be Uncle Milton. The moment you go outside, you'll be the DA."

Milton stared at her. "If I don't do what needs to be done, many will suffer. I'm the only one who can help the people of this county," he said and then walked out of the church, his footfalls echoing in the sanctuary.

The moment he exited, the protesters roared once again.

Paul wanted to look out the window to see how much their numbers had grown but feared making a sound. Instead he remained on the floor peering over the balcony railing. Anne knelt with her head down. He couldn't tell if she was weeping or praying.

Comments on the Thebes Weekly website:

1. There's a great danger in believing you alone are right. The one who thinks that, who maintains that only he has the power to reason correctly, a man like that, when you know him, turns out empty.

2. Will nobody here listen to reason, or is everyone just obsessed with being unreasonable?

3. This is politics at its worst. This county deserves what it gets. When the spirit of the law is broken like this, this county will fall. Anarchy, baby! Bad things will come of this.

4. Where is Susan Doyle?

5. Reply: She's still in the hospital. She got messed up pretty bad. Look, I'm pro-choice and everything, but I think that clinic sucks.

6. So is he going to let her off? Is the law for everyone or only a select few? For us regular people? But if you're politically connected then you're fine. Jeez, what God did this family piss off? They seem cursed!

7. When the laws are kept, the city stands! When the laws are broken, what of our city then? Never may the anarchist find rest.

37

"Anti-gay scum!"

"Child abuser!"

The mob hurled insults at Fr. Quinn from behind the yellow tape as he walked to the church from the rectory. One voice yelled out "Abettor!", but that failed to catch on with the crowd.

Another chant became the instant fan favorite: "Peeeeedo! Peeeeeedo! Peeeeeedo!"

Since the clergy abuse scandal broke in the early 2000s, "Peeeedo" became the go-to slam against any and all priests. That word cut to Fr. Quinn's heart. In this present darkness, the cross many priests were forced to carry was the reputation of the Church itself, which had often concealed, obfuscated, and lied about the abuse crisis for decades. Nearly everything he wanted to be as a shepherd of souls was undercut by the crimes of people running his beloved Church.

He didn't even realize he was shaking until he held up his hand to wave ironically and smile at the angry protesters. He stopped himself as he spotted Michael Olden against the yellow tape and turned his wave into a blessing for the old man, which enraged the activists further.

Once inside the church, he scanned the pews until he saw Anne kneeling before a statue of the Blessed Virgin, her head tilted up in prayer. Fr. Quinn approached her, sat in the front pew behind her, and waited. Eventually, she turned and joined him in the pew.

"Thank you for coming," she said. "We should probably do this now. I don't know how long I have."

Looking at her, it was easy to forget that she was surrounded by police and an angry crowd outside. Fr. Quinn nodded solemnly, walked up the middle aisle, genuflected at the foot of the altar, then disappeared into the sanctuary. He returned moments later wearing a plain purple cassock.

The chants outside escalated, but Anne seemed only to hear the priest.

She approached him and laid the tiny bundle in a white blanket at the foot of the sanctuary. Father Quinn nodded, caught a lump in his throat, approached the tabernacle, then dropped to his knees and spread his arms. "The perpetual mercy of God desires that all be saved, and this should give us hope," he said, his voice echoing throughout the church. "Please recall Jesus said 'Let the children come to me, do not hinder them.' Heavenly Father, you saved the world through your Son, Jesus Christ. You saw your only Son on the cross and forgave this sinful world. Please baptize this child with the Precious blood and water in the name of the Father and of the Son and of the Holy Spirit. May this child through Jesus Christ gain everlasting life, through his wounds be healed, and through his precious blood be freed."

"Amen," Anne said.

Fr. Quinn stepped up to the podium and read from the Book of Wisdom. "But the souls of the just are in the hand of God, and no torment shall touch them. They seemed, in the view of the foolish, to be dead; and their passing away was thought an affliction and their going forth from us, utter destruction. But they are in peace. For if before people, indeed, they be punished, yet is their hope full of immortality; chastised a little, they shall be greatly blessed, because God tried them and found them worthy of himself. As gold in the furnace, he proved them, and as sacrificial offerings he took them to himself. In the time of their visitation they shall shine, and shall dart about as sparks through stubble; they shall judge nations and rule over peoples, and the Lord shall be their King forever. Those who trust in God shall understand truth, and the faithful shall abide with him in love: because grace and mercy are with his holy ones, and God's care is with the elect."

At the responsorial psalm, Anne bowed her head. "The Lord is my shepherd," she said. "There is nothing I shall want."

Paul, listening from the balcony above, wondered about that. "There is nothing I shall want." He'd heard it before but never really considered it. He always took it as saying, "If I'm a Christian, God will give me everything I want." A childish notion, easily disprovable. But suddenly it struck him differently. It wasn't making a demand on God but on oneself. In fact, it wasn't about getting what one wanted from God; it was about reprioritizing what one wanted. It was saying, "God is enough. I crave only God." Why hadn't anyone explained that to him before?

"Christ has died," Anne said. "Christ is risen. Christ will come again."

Paul, crouched on the balcony and watched Fr. Quinn lift the Eucharist in the air, his arms extended. "Take this, all of you, and eat of it, for this is my body, which will be given up for you." Repeating this with a chalice, Fr. Quinn held it aloft. "Take this, all of you, and drink from it, for this is the chalice of my blood, the blood of the new and eternal covenant that will be poured out for you and for many for the forgiveness of sins. Do this in memory of me."

With the sun shining through the stained glass, Anne approached to receive the Body of Christ, knelt at the altar rail, her eyes on the Eucharist, and received it on her tongue.

A question struck Paul: What if it all were true?

No.

But his thoughts tumbled in anyway. *What if it is true? What if God did create the world as an act of love? Is that so farfetched? Nobody knows how everything began, right? And scientifically, we do know something can't come from nothing. So we either believe the universe always existed, or there's a creator, right?*

And if—big if—if there is a creator, that . . . entity must have certain feelings toward creation, right? Does it make sense to create and abandon?

Thinking of his own parents, he had always known that wasn't how it should've been. He wished it hadn't been. So, if a Creator loved his creation, would he be willing to allow his Son to die in order to show the world how much he loved them? Didn't that make sense? What had all seemed like superstition seemed to make some sense. And yet, Paul remained unwilling to make that leap. No way.

But why did his parents' actions seem so . . . wrong to him? What could be deemed "wrong" anyway? How did we all agree on "wrong" and "right"? And if there was an objective right and wrong, where did it they come from?

His head hurt.

But why did Anne seem so confident in all of it? He wanted to rush down and ask her why she believed, why her belief remained so unshaken that she'd put her life in danger. But he stayed hidden, crawling along the floor and unable to stand for fear of being seen.

Concluding the Mass, Fr. Quinn raised an aspergillum, a silver ball on a wooden stick, and sprinkled holy water on the tiny white bundle at the foot of the sanctuary. "As a sign of the dignity of the body of the deceased and of our hope that by the power of the Holy Spirit they have been raised to eternal life," he said.

They both heard the church door push open and turned to see a skinny priest in black with thinning hair and a hawk-like nose explode inside.

38

"FATHER QUINN?" THE THIN priest said as he proceeded up the aisle. "I'm with Bishop Stolic's office. My name is Father Stephen Spadaro. He commands your presence downtown." When Fr. Quinn didn't move, he added, "Immediately, Father."

Anne lifted the bundle, genuflected, and stepped toward the front pew.

"Um," Fr. Quinn said, looking over at Anne, "I don't know what to do."

"Father, go. Please. I'll be OK," Anne implored.

"Hmmph," Fr. Spadaro said. "Who exactly are you taking orders from now, the bishop or this young lady?"

Fr. Quinn approached Anne. "I should've expected this," he whispered. "I'll be back as soon as I can, and we'll figure this out."

He stepped down from the sanctuary and lifted his cassock off, under which he wore his black shirt and white priestly collar. He laid his cassock on the front pew next to Anne. "Anne," Fr. Quinn said. "Look at me. Don't leave until I get back. Promise me. We'll figure this out."

"A car is waiting for you," Fr. Spadaro said curtly, now standing within inches of Fr. Quinn. "I'll stay here."

"Anne," Fr. Quinn, whispered, "perhaps the bishop can work something out. Perhaps when I get back, this will all be solved."

"Perhaps," Anne said. "Thank you for the Mass."

Fr. Spadaro cleared his throat theatrically and followed closely behind Fr. Quinn. At the door, Fr. Quinn turned back. "Do you know what the bishop wants?"

"Bishop Stolic requested I come here and . . . fetch you. As an obedient priest, I did as he asked."

Fr. Quinn half smiled, getting the unsubtle message. At the door he turned and took one more look at Anne, then turned back to Fr. Spadaro. "Please take care of her."

137

"A priest's charge is to care for the entire flock," Fr. Spadaro said, "not pick favorites."

Fr. Quinn locked eyes with Anne.

"Go," she urged, and he walked out. The crowd roared upon seeing him.

"Peeedo! Peeeeeeedo! Peeeedo!"

39

FR. QUINN HAD A gift for not planning. It left him almost irreversibly content because he rarely worried about the future. Members of the parish council sometimes felt they were left to do all the worrying (and working), but most of them loved Fr. Quinn and wanted to protect him from the consequences of his administrative shortcomings, although even their patience faltered when he attended an event he had hardly worked on and announced, "See? The Holy Spirit made it all come together despite your worries." Margaret, the council's vice president, would sometimes whisper in the kitchen that it wasn't just the Holy Spirit.

Fr. Quinn hadn't planned to allow Anne to declare sanctuary in the church, but in his heart, he believed that if he just made the right decision, everything would work out. He'd heard stories about the bishop being hardnosed and ambitious, but the pictures in the paper always portrayed him smiling or throwing his head back in laughter. Looking at those, Fr. Quinn had long thought they would get along well. In fact, he daydreamed for a moment that the two would get along so well that he'd be appointed to some commission in Rome, which he would turn down in order to remain a parish priest.

He had met the bishop once when he'd lectured at seminary on "Spiritualization of Matter—as demonstrated by Paleontology." After the talk, they gathered in a conference room for hors d'oeuvres. The bishop glided about the room speaking to the seminarians. He found Fr. Quinn—then merely Peter—near the pizza rolls. "I enjoyed your talk immensely, your Excellency," Peter said. "Very enlightening."

Bishop Stolic smiled to the two priests accompanying him around the room. "And what exactly did you find so enlightening?" he asked.

Oh noooooooooooo! Peter sought for a coherent thought.

"Don't worry," the bishop said, patting his arm before walking away. "Teilhard de Chardin isn't for everyone."

Fr. Quinn blushed at the memory. He googled the bishop in order to easily make conversation with him. The *Philadelphia Daily News* described him as "The smiling face of the American Church." The most frequent picture of him in the news showed him standing between the Phillies mascot, the Fanatic, and the mayor.

When the bishop was a campus minister at Saint Joseph's University in Philadelphia, he created a student club to deliver food to needy people in the community, specifically Islamic refugees. When asked by a journalist if he was trying to convert the Muslims, he wrapped his arm around one of the refugees and said, "I'm not doing this to make him a Catholic. I'm doing this because I am one." Fr. Quinn didn't know what to make of that. He turned his phone off and looked out the window and prayed that God would give him the words.

Fr. Quinn entered the bishop's residence and was led up the stairs by a short gray-haired woman who had trouble lifting her right leg up the stairs, so she leaned heavily on the banister. Fr. Quinn asked about her leg, and she widened her eyes not only as if he'd said something that shocked her but also as if his very ability to speak surprised her. Wordlessly, she trudged up the final few steps and opened the heavy office door. Fr. Quinn thanked her as she backed up and closed the door behind him.

He glanced around the office. Plants! Everywhere. Wow. Spilling out of plant holders. Hanging from the ceiling. Sitting on the huge wooden desk. Standing on every inch of windowsill. Green. He looked around and found Bishop Timothy Stolic standing in the corner of his office emitting a mist from a green bottle over a big-leafed plant whose leaves overflowed its purple plant holder. *Squirt. Squirt. Squirt.*

Bishop Stolic didn't even glance up as Fr. Quinn entered with his hands clasped in front of him. Unsure where to go, he stood nervously behind a chair. He didn't know if he should speak, so he watched the bishop meticulously and carefully lift leaves and vines and squirt the soil underneath. He didn't miss a spot. He expected the bishop to acknowledge him eventually, but instead the bishop continued, moving on to a plant that stood three feet tall next to a bookshelf containing more plants.

Squirt. The bishop appeared to be deciding whether to spray more, tilted his head one way, then another, and finally looked over his reading glasses at Fr. Quinn. "Sit, Peter," he said.

"Thank you, your excellency," Fr. Quinn said and sat on the edge of a plastic chair with green cushions, his back straight. "Your office is—"

"This is being recorded for your protection," the bishop said, taking his seat behind the desk.

Fr. Quinn wondered for the first time if he was not there to be given help. But why? His mind searched for answers. Were they looking for someone to blame? Were they covering themselves legally?

"Let's start this off. Father Quinn, tell me about how you feel the parish is going. Tell me some of the initiatives of which you're most proud."

For a moment, Father Quinn fostered the insane idea that perhaps this meeting wasn't about Anne at all. He told the bishop about his work with the youth group, organizing busses to attend the March for Life every January and his work with the soup kitchen on Saturday mornings.

"This is exactly what I expected when you were assigned this parish just two years ago," the bishop said. "I did not, however, expect what's occurring now."

"Me neither," Fr. Quinn said, forcing a smile that the bishop didn't return.

"Let's cut to it, shall we? You and this young woman, was this the plan all along? Is there something . . . between you two that we should discuss?

"No, your excellency, of course not."

"But you know her?"

"She's a parishioner. Active. Attends mass a few times a week."

"An extremist? Fundamentalist?"

"No, your excellency. I don't even know what that word means in this context."

"Hmm . . . Did she make you aware of her intentions beforehand?

"No."

"You presided at her father's funeral? Yes? And did she speak to you?"

"Yes, but only to thank me. An awkward moment did occur though."

"With this Anne person?"

"Not exactly. Susan Doyle left before I arrived. Susan is the woman—"

"The news has made us all painfully aware who she is," the bishop said.

"Anyway, your excellency, when Anne's sister, Izzy, spat in her face, I'm not sure how many people saw it, but Susan Doyle understandably left shortly after. I would've liked to have spoken with her, but she is not a parishioner, and I didn't learn about this until later."

The bishop brought his hands together in front of his face as he considered his words. "So, to be clear, your parishioners are spitting in the faces of pregnant women and forcing their way into women's health clinics, stealing biological material, and then hiding in your parish. As you sit here, your parish is surrounded by police, and parishioners are unable to attend Mass. Oh yes, and it's all televised for the world to see."

"Your excellency, all this has happened in the past few days," Fr. Quinn said. "The past two years have gone well."

"Oh, would you like to count the number of days pregnant women haven't been shamed in your parish? Or the days you haven't made the church an accomplice to a crime or the center of a national media circus?" He tilted his head exaggeratedly to make clear the question was rhetorical. The bishop closed his eyes and inhaled deeply. ,"I don't want this to be an emotional meeting. Do you?"

"Um, what?"

"I want to be clearheaded here. I'm going to turn the recorder off. Is that OK with you?"

"Yes, your excellency."

"I find that at times like these, honesty is often the best policy. Do you believe that?

"Yes, your ex—"

Bishop Stolic reached out to a plant on the left side of his desk. The edge of one leaf at the top of the plant had turned slightly yellow, its edges brown. He took hold of the stem and yanked the mottled leaf off. He rolled it in the fingers of his right hand and leaned back. "Father Quinn, when I came here four years ago, the archdiocese was swimming in over seventy million dollars of debt, several Catholic schools just closed, and we were teetering on the brink of bankruptcy. Do you know what that means?" Fr. Quinn thought the question might be rhetorical, so he just stared at the bishop. "It means all the services we provide to the poor would be cut. Every scholarship to poor and minority children would be drastically reduced or revoked. Parishes sold off. I have spent long nights planning and praying for a way forward. And right now, due to the clergy abuse scandals, many don't trust priests or the Church. The Church in America exists on a precipice, on dangerous ground. But I believe that here we've made some strides to put the Church on stable footing.

"Um, I think what you've done is amazing," Fr. Quinn said, thinking a compliment would serve him well.

Bishop Stolic acted like he hadn't even heard him. "Peter, would you agree the Church needs healing and the way forward must bring people together?"

"Yes," Fr. Quinn replied, glad to offer a firm response.

"But what's happening in your parish right now, something like this divides us. It . . . tears. This is not the time for division. You have . . . *we* have a situation in your parish that is tearing the community apart. Police surround your church holding back protesters. A criminal is hiding in your parish, and faithful parishioners can't even attend Mass. All on national television. You understand this situation is calamitous, correct?"

"Yes, your excellency."

"And the ramifications aren't contained to your parish. The entire archdiocese is affected. And in the end, this hurts those whom the Church helps. It hurts parishes Catholic schools. And Father Quinn, what about all those post-abortive women in search of healing? After something like this plays out on every television, women are far less likely to seek out the Church for healing. So, it is precisely those whom we seek to help who are most hurt by your actions."

"My actions?" Fr. Quinn said, incredulous. "I just tried to help a young woman and—"

"Let's assume that's true," Bishop Stolic said, holding out his hands. "I think sometimes when looking at a situation it helps to look to Jesus, who said, 'You shall know them by their fruits.' And I think if we're looking at the consequences of your actions, we can see that it's poisonous fruit. I think that's fair to say, don't you?"

Fr. Quinn shifted in his seat as Bishop Stolic continued. "I believe the wise thing to do for the good of the Church, for the poor, for all the children the Church helps provide for, we must ask this young woman to leave the church."

"You want me to tell her to leave?"

"Peter," Bishop Stolic said as if he were saying something everyone in the world knew to be true, "the girl must leave the church."

"I know that your excellency," Fr. Quinn said. "I do."

"You know that yet every action you've taken has guaranteed the opposite reality," he said. "She must leave now. Father Quinn, will you order her to leave immediately?"

"Your excellency," Fr. Quinn said, "she wished to have a funeral, and I thought the unborn deserved that. I have fulfilled that wish. I believe she was planning to go outside just when you brought me here."

"Ah, so this is my fault?"

"No, no, your excellency," Fr. Quinn sputtered. "I'm just saying I think her intention is to leave now although—"

"Although what?" Bishop Stolic leaned forward, head tilted.

"She hasn't said this specifically, but I believe that when she walks out of the church, she intends to bury the remains in the cemetery."

The bishop's eyes widened, and he leaned back in his chair as if his desk were on fire. "And you want to allow this?"

"I believe—as we all do—that every life is sacred and deserving of our respect and—"

"Are you insane?" the words erupted from the bishop, his face reddening and his eyes bulging. "You want to stage a burial on Church property in the middle of a national firestorm? And you want a criminal to literally bury the evidence of her crime in front of the world? And you want me to approve this?"

"I didn't think of it like that. I just thought it would be a good—"

"You thought? You *thought*?" the bishop yelled but quickly gathered himself and placed his hands on his desk. His next words were measured. "Father Quinn, I'm asking, what would you have me do?"

Fr. Quinn remained silent, unsure if he should answer.

"Well, as your bishop I am ordering you to evict that criminal from the parish right now."

"Oh," Fr. Quinn said, wide eyed.

"Will you comply with my order?" Bishop Stolic asked. The phrasing of the question indicated the stakes. Canon law allowed the bishop to reassign a pastor for "the good of souls or the necessity or advantage of the Church."

Bishop Stolic pushed his phone across the desk. "Call Father Spadaro, and order Anne Prince to leave the church. If she refuses, we will call the police to have her evicted. I have spoken to the district attorney. They are awaiting our call."

Fr. Quinn's face turned white. He couldn't believe he was about to ask what he was about to ask. "And just to be clear, I don't mean to be, umm . . . antagonistic, but what happens if I don't?"

"I will have no choice but to reassign you to a more suitable role, and Ms. Prince will be ordered to leave the church by Father Spadaro. Either way, she's out. The only question is whether you stay in your parish."

Fr. Quinn looked at the floor, sick to his stomach. Could he throw Anne out? What about his role as pastor?

The bishop extended his arms and laid his hands flat on his desk. "Father Quinn," he said in a conciliatory tone, "you've done some excellent work out there. Previous to this week I'd heard wonderful things about you. Many of your parishioners foster a deep affection toward you. Do you want to abandon them to be assigned to clerical duties in the seminary? Would that aid their spiritual life? What about yours? You're a shepherd of souls. That is your vocation. Do not abandon your flock. Think of the soup kitchen and the youth group. Who knows what will happen to them without your guidance?"

Bishop Stolic pushed his phone across the desk. Fr. Spadaro's number was already in the phone. Fr. Quinn hesitated, closed his eyes, and pushed "send."

40

Bzzzzz. Bzzzz.

The noise came from behind Anne. *Bzzz.* Father Spadaro brought his phone to his ear. Anne, still kneeling, looked at him sprawled in the pew.

"Helloooo Father Quinn," the priest said playfully. "I was expecting your call."

Fr. Quinn's voice over the phone was a whisper. "Hello."

"We've been waiting. Do you have something to say? You're on speaker." He pushed the volume button and held his phone out just inches from Anne's face as she stared forward at the crucifix above the altar.

"Anne?"

"Yes, Father."

Silence.

"It's OK, Father," Anne said with understanding and sympathy in her voice. "Just say it."

A long silence. "Anne, I called to tell you to leave the parish."

Anne barely reacted. Father Spadaro raised his one eyebrow and smiled crookedly as Fr. Quinn continued. "Anne, I can't do it. There are a million reasons to do it, but it's not the right thing. A shepherd must leave the flock to chase even one lost sheep. That is my vocation. I will not ask you to leave the church. It won't be me."

Anne smiled, and tears welled in her eyes.

Father Spadaro's smile vanished, and he hung up the phone. "OK," he said. "As the new acting pastor of St. Stephen the Martyr Parish, madam, I'm afraid I must order you to leave this building."

Anne's face registered no surprise. She genuflected, blessed herself, and pulled on her red coat. Fr. Spadaro stepped back from her.

Anne gathered the white blanket tenderly in the crook of her right arm and walked to the door. He couldn't allow her to leave without a parting shot. "Your type of Catholics are holding the Church back!" he yelled, his voice shaking with more emotion than he intended. "You fundamentalists, you prioritize dogma over love of neighbor. You're what's wrong with the Church. You smear us all with your intolerance."

"This is my neighbor too," Anne said, looking at the bundle in her arms. She turned away, holding the white blanket close to her chest.

"Anne, don't go!" Paul called out from the balcony. "I think I can get you out of here."

41

MILTON STOOD ON THE steps of the church in front of the press. The crowd pressed up against the police to hear every word. He appeared sharp, calm, and decisive even as his sternum shook. He inhaled. This was the moment that would decide his political career. The cable news channels ran their "Breaking News" chyrons and went live to Saint Stephen the Martyr's Parish for an update.

"This egregious attack on female reproductive health is not only an embarrassment to the entire state of Pennsylvania but, more importantly, it jeopardizes the health and well-being of pregnant women everywhere," Milton said. "Stunts like this make it more difficult and more painful for women to access health care and are yet another politically motivated attack on women's rights by some on the extreme right. It intentionally makes life harder for those seeking care. And sadly, that's the point."

The protesters cheered. Emboldened, he continued. "A clearly doctored video purporting to show illegal dumping of biological remains has now been debunked and banned by social media. Meant to embarrass law-abiding women who are exercising their constitutional rights, it is a deeply cynical strategy and an affront to settled law. I am instructing police that the district attorney's office will file charges immediately, and if police place Anne Prince under arrest, the district attorney's office will have her in front of a judge tonight."

Raucous cheers. The protesters looked at each other wide eyed to confirm what they were hearing.

"My heart . . . my heart . . . my heart . . ." The cheers were too loud and sustained for him to complete his sentence. He waited. "My heart breaks for Anne Prince, who is clearly in need of help. I love my niece, but we are a nation built on law. If we fail to enforce some laws due to familial entanglements or heartstrings, we risk anarchy. I understand from our conversation that my niece, Anne Prince, believes in the rightness of what she's doing. She believes God's law supersedes man's law." He expected the crowd to go silent at that point but quickly added a "however" to turn it around. "We live in a pluralistic society, one that does not allow adherents of one particular religion to force their beliefs on others or to stigmatize those who disagree. That is not how we live here in Pennsylvania or in America at large. Tolerance must be our north star. Inclusion must be the banner we march under.

"This is a time when our nation is split. This country needs to come together. And we cannot abide by some demonizing others to further their political agenda. Any movement whose strategy is making women feel terrible about an already excruciating decision has no place at the table of civil discourse. That time has gone. If this country wants to progress, we must . . . do what is right, even when it's difficult. Especially when it's difficult."

He paused. The crowd cheered, quieted, and waited for his next words. He had them. Oh, the thrill of it. The power. And it was all being televised. Nationally!

"We must all act for the greater good. We must no longer be a country of individuals but an individual country, standing together, strong, united. For too long the wheels of justice have run over Americans. Those who seek to weaponize our politics must be resisted."

The crowd erupted and pushed forward, the yellow tape reaching the limits of its elasticity. Milton raised his hands as if to say that's not what he intended, but the shouts drowned him out. The crowd surged forward, inspired by the proximity of the cameras. Within moments, the police tape lay torn and trampled, and the officers plummeted into the midst of the crowd.

The cable news channels did not cut to commercial break but spun the cameras around.

42

"WHO'S THERE? COME OUT!" Fr. Spadaro yelled, his head whipping around in search of the voice.

Paul stood at the edge of the balcony, his legs unsteady and his left leg tingling from crouching for so long. "Don't go, Anne," he said, his hands on the rail.

She stopped and looked up at him.

"Don't go! Please."

She stepped forward, smiling. "I'm grateful, Paul. I'm touched. I know you didn't come here to try to save me. You came for the story, right?"

He hesitated briefly and searched for a word to sum up all the mixed-up thoughts and conflicts in his mind. "Yes. I don't know how else to say it but yes. But now I'm thinking, forget the story. Forget it all. Please don't go out there."

He shook his right leg and stumbled toward the stairs, afraid she would walk out the door. He heard Anne laugh as he hopped.

"Anne, listen. Everything's different now. I don't even know how or why. I just know I don't give a damn about the story. Everything that seemed important to me . . . doesn't now. When I came here I wanted the story. That's it. But now . . . Izzy asked me to come here and help and that's what I intend to do.

"I'm so touched," she said. "I really am."

"Anne, wait until tonight," Paul said. "I think we can sneak out."

"Where did you come from?" Fr. Spadaro interjected. "Are you with the press? How long have you been here?"

Paul figured Fr. Spadaro was trying to remember if he'd said anything that could be used against him.

"Paul is with the press," Anne said. "He came in late last night, actually around two thirty this morning."

"You knew?" Paul asked.

"Izzy texted me you were coming and . . . you're not as sneaky as you thought, but that's probably a good thing." She smiled. "Maybe there's hope for you yet."

Fr. Spadaro turned toward the far wall and dialed a number on his phone, initiating a whispered conversation.

Paul thought of the door the undertakers had come through. He didn't know where it went, but he thought it might lead out to an exit left uncovered by police or at least by the mob. Either way, he'd snuck in the night before. Perhaps he could sneak her out.

The crowd noise swelled outside. Each of them glanced at the window but couldn't see anything.

Still smiling, Anne turned back to Paul. "Thank you, but I believe I'm going where I need to." She walked toward the door.

"Whoa. Whoa. Hold on," Paul said, holding out his hands over the balcony railing. "I'm just confused right now."

"About what?" she asked. "You've been here. You know everything. So, what are you confused about?"

He searched for an answer, words to prevent her from leaving. "Why? I guess I just don't get why?"

"Paul, you know why. I believe every life is sacred. I believe God created the world as an act of love, and we should respect creation as a gift. *All* creation. I was born to join in love, not hate. That's my nature. *Our* nature. And no matter what law is passed by man, we must answer to a higher law."

"But . . . is it true?" Paul asked.

"Truth isn't always something you can explain," she said. "Sometimes you have to feel it. Come down from the balcony to where the miracles happen. Miracles are messy. Sometimes you have to get your hands dirty. Stop writing about people, Paul, and become one!"

"Anne, Izzy would kill me if I let you go outside," he said, not knowing what else to say.

"Take care of her," she said. " Now that you know everything, go tell the world. Maybe that's what all this has been for. Maybe my part is over. Maybe it's up to you now."

She looked tired, but her blue eyes still burned.

Fr. Spadaro rushed past Anne and pushed open the door. "Bishop Stolic says you must vacate the church immediately!"

She faced the open door. "Your will be done," she said, then stepped outside.

43

PAUL KNEW THE FEAR of crowds or mobs was called enochlophobia or eemophobia. People tended to think of it as an irrational fear. However, it seemed perfectly rational to fear an angry mob. It was interesting that many times, the more humans assembled for a cause, the less humanely they acted. In fact, there seemed to be something in humans that recoiled at the sight of an overwhelming and irrational physical presence.

Looking out from the balcony window, Paul saw the police officers overwhelmed and separated. He saw Milton Prince working against the crowd, trying to get around it like a linebacker sidestepping an offensive line with his arms making a swimming motion. As he attempted to work his way through the crowd away from the church steps, he was pushed closer all the time with each surge of the crowd until he stood with his back to the stone wall and his arms across the front of his body.

The crowd reached the steps of the church just as Anne stepped blinking into the daylight. When they saw her before them in the doorway, they stopped. Nobody had expected this. Hundreds of angry men and women, mostly young, many wearing masks, stared. Even the three police officers stopped. Some protesters near the back of the crowd, wearing satanic horns, looked confusedly at each other. The majority of news cameras filmed everything from a safe distance, but some rushed around to the other side of the crowd to get a clearer shot of Anne.

The police officers took advantage of the momentary pause and pushed their way toward the front of the group. This woke the crowd again, which surrounded, jostled, and shoved them. Officer Hardaway didn't even know who punched him in the side of the face, but the blow struck his temple and staggered him. When Hardaway raised a police club above his shoulder, a tall man wearing an Orioles baseball hat and a blue scarf wrapped around his lower face grabbed it from behind and pulled it from his grip. Hardaway yelled, and Officer Dougherty and a twenty eight-year-old female officer named Deborah Stinson lowered their shoulders and pushed toward him. Stinson ducked low and ran toward the man with the club and sprayed something in his face. His Orioles hat flew off his head as he dropped the club and brought his hands to his eyes. The man screamed and fell back, and the spray hit others who whirled and screamed. Others wearing goggles or sunglasses reacted by squeezing in around the police. The cacophony swelled, and the police disappeared into the surging mass of humanity.

Anne, carrying her bundle close to her chest, descended the steps unnoticed by the crowd, which had focused its ire on the three police officers. She turned toward the cemetery gate, and for a moment Paul nurtured the insane thought that she might just walk out of there untouched like a cartoon character out of a cloud of adversaries.

But a man in a denim jacket over a hooded sweatshirt with a red do-rag over his lower face lunged forward, his black boots bouncing, approaching Anne from the side.

"Watch out!" Paul yelled and banged his hands on the church window, but nobody heard him. Anne never even looked toward the approaching man until he howled and raised a red bike lock over his head and swung it savagely at Anne's head just above her ear. She collapsed hard, and her head hit the ground in an unnerving way.

Unmoving, Paul's vision was filled with his own reflection in the large window, but he looked past it toward Anne. He watched, frozen, as her hands didn't even extend to break her fall, and the white cloth she held in her arms dropped onto the sidewalk.

"Yeah, bitch!" Todd Dooley yelled in a high-pitched squeal. "Yeeee-aaaaaahhhh!" That got the crowd's attention. They spotted him, then Anne, and then the little bundle on the concrete next to her.

The silence didn't begin immediately. It took a few moments. Those nearest to Anne gasped and stepped back. The people behind them peered over their shoulders and recoiled. Others filled in, only to bring their hands to their mouths or close their eyes.

They saw Anne lying there with blood pouring from her head. The white blanket was open on the concrete. At the end of one arm was a tiny hand. With fingers. Fingers! And a face. Everyone could see it. A face! Misshapen and torn apart but a baby's face. It looked like it was experiencing a fitful nightmare. The legs, one of them lying above the sternum and the other below, were bent in the way knees are bent. It looked so . . . human.

The cameramen and women rushed in, unsure what they were even filming, focusing their cameras on Anne sprawled on the concrete and the menacing figure with a bike lock looming over her. When they saw the scattered limbs, they swirled their cameras back to the crowd.

Silence.

When Anne shifted on the ground, the cameras focused on her once again, their lights causing her to squint. She raised herself with one arm, looked confusedly at the crowd and her attacker. She glanced back toward the church as if remembering why she was there, closed her eyes, locked her elbow, and lifted herself off the ground. She wavered, unsure of her balance.

Many in the crowd gasped. They hadn't expected her to get up. Still wobbling, she looked at the crowd in front of her and spotted Michael Olden, who lifted the police tape, stepped under it, and walked to her.

"God loves you, Anne," he said, holding his rosary.

She smiled and mouthed the words "Thank you."

"Please allow me to help you," he said, crouching on one knee and tenderly assembled the remains in the white blanket. He stood and handed the bundle to Anne.

"God bless you," she said as she accepted the blanket.

"God loves you, Anne," he said and then backed away.

Anne held the white blanket up in front of the crowd. "This is my brother!" she proclaimed.

The protesters responded with a guttural shriek, a cacophony of rage. The crowd surged forward, bellying up to Anne, their screaming faces contorted in anger. Paul saw Michael pulled down from behind. He zoomed in with his phone camera but didn't see him again.

He searched again for Anne but couldn't locate her in the crowd. Had something happened to her? He couldn't just stand there. He couldn't.

He took the steps two at a time and raced out the doors to find Anne.

Paul was pulled roughly back by two men in black hoodies. "You're with her?" they asked. Before he even had time to respond, one punched him in the chest. "You came from inside the church! He's with Anne Prince!"

Paul saw several other protesters nearby look their way.

"Yeah, he must have been in there with her!" one woman yelled as she approached.

"No, no, no, I'm a journalist," Paul said. "I'm covering the story for the San Francisco Reporter."

"Bullshit," someone said.

Others gathered around, one holding a bat. Somebody grabbed his collar from behind and shook him. "Nazi bastard."

A jolt of fear made Paul's knees buckle. "I'm a journalist. Look. Look." Panicked, he reached into his wallet to pull out his press identification, but his hands were shaking so badly he spilled its contents on the steps. He dropped to his knees in the middle of the crowd and searched the cards. When he found his press identification he held it over his head. "Press!" he screeched. "I'm a journalist. I'm not with her."

The crowd around him laughed that his voice had cracked. But they let go of his collar and backed away from the church steps. One of them imitated him, screaming, "Press! Press!", and they all laughed.

Paul sat there alone. He looked toward the graveyard and saw Anne walking toward it surrounded by masked men and women waving pipes, bats, and sticks behind her.

Comments on the WXPR News website, which had broken into live coverage:

1. Way too far. This has become a national spectacle. Too daring—smashing against the high throne of justice!

2. Your life's in ruins, child—I wonder . . . are you paying for your father's terrible ordeal?

3. Anne Prince has gone too far. And now she's literally fighting City Hall. She will lose. Child, you'll be ruined. Guaranteed. The sins of the father are visited on the daughter.

4. This girl is a tornado. She will rage, and people will be hurt. Mark my words.

5. The oh so mighty words of the proud will be paid in full. Everyone just please chill out. Seriously! Everyone involved here is just too proud. Time and life will teach you wisdom.

44

THE POLICE OFFICERS EMERGED together on the far side of the crowd with their arms interlocked, yelling into their radios strapped to their shirts. Officer Stinson, bleeding from her face, stumbled along with their assistance. Together they made their way to an ambulance parked near the rectory.

With Stinson inside the vehicle, Paul saw Dougherty yelling into the radio while Hardaway limped in circles with his hands on his hips. They weren't going back in.

Anne was alone.

Cameramen and women walked the fence line of the graveyard with their lights trained on Anne. The protesters crowded around her, shouting "Bitch!" and "Nazi."

Just as Anne entered the graveyard, a rock slammed into the iron archway just above her head so loudly that some thought the bell in the tower had sounded for the first time in years. *Gong!* The reporters took a few steps back. Some in the crowd liked the sound and reached up to bang rocks against the top of the archway. *Gong. Gong. Gong.*

Anne stepped forward, and another rock hit her in the side. She arched backward in pain but didn't fall. Even some in the crowd groaned. Others yelled like someone had just scored in a highlight reel.

Gong.

The crowd followed behind her shouting and cursing, their faces twisted in anger. Some on the outskirts of the pack climbed over the low gate to approach. Anne zigzagged around the tombstones as some in the crowd dashed forward to reach out and push her, as if to check if there would be any consequences, then fell back into the anonymity of the crowd. When nothing happened, they grew bolder.

Gong.

One woman with purple hair and goggles ran up and smacked Anne in the back of the head and raised her arms triumphantly. The crowd responded with laughter.

Along the graveyard fence, a group of reporters recorded everything with their phones. To Paul's left, a solitary figure stood on the steps of the church. Milton Prince took a step toward Anne and the graveyard, but the young man who followed him everywhere approached him and spoke in his ear. After one last look toward Anne, the two turned and jogged toward the rectory parking lot. Milton never looked back.

Gong.

When Paul turned his attention back to Anne, he saw a large piece of wood flying high over the crowd from the rear, so high that Paul had time to wonder why someone brought a two-by-four to a protest. It hurtled end over end and struck Anne in the lower back. The crowd roared as if a trick shot has just been scored, and Anne fell to her knees.

One man with a baseball hat, sunglasses, and a beard rushed forward., "Stop!" he yelled. "This is what they want. Don't give in to violence!" But he was pushed back into the crowd.

Anne rose, slower this time, using the piece of wood to balance herself momentarily.

Gong.

She stepped forward to an open area between gravestones and knelt in the dirt. She leaned forward as the crowd watched her. She reached forward and plunged her hands into the dirt. Dust flew from the dry ground creating a light haze around her.

It took a moment for many to conceive of her intentions. "She's burying the body!" someone yelled. The outrage exploded into an apocalyptic thunder, and the crowd tightened around her, their knees against her side. The exhalations of the crowd peaked in volume and intensity. Someone threw a sign saying, "My life, My Choice" like a Frisbee, but it sailed over everyone's heads and landed harmlessly against a gravestone.

Gong.

Paul could no longer see Anne from his vantage point in front of the church, so he stood, abandoning the contents of his wallet scattered on the church steps. He could no longer see Anne through the crowd and the dust, so he ran the length of the fence, entered the graveyard, and wove through the gravestones.

Through the bramble of limbs, he saw her on her knees, her arms clawing at the earth. Another rock flew past her head and skipped past several gravestones. A man on the left of the crowd wearing goggles and a hoodie threw a small rock he had taken off the top of a tombstone, hitting Anne's feet.

Paul screamed, but nobody heard him.

Anne lay on her stomach but rose again to her knees where she lifted up the remains of her brother in the white blanket and laid them in the small hole she'd created. She blessed herself and then pushed the dirt over the body.

A figure stepped close to her, blocking out the sun. She looked at the dark outline. The denim-and-leather-clad man in the mask with the red bike lock stood over her once again, his wide shoulders rising and falling. "Nazi scum!" he screamed and grabbed her hair, twisting it, and pulling her away from the tiny bundle. Even as she was lifted she reached out to cover the tiny body and even kicked at the dirt with her feet.

He slammed her down a few feet away.

Anne turned over, and the two stared at each other. She said something that Paul couldn't hear. The man backed up a step, and Anne took the opportunity to reach out with her hands to pull more dirt onto the remains. The man screamed as he raised his arm. In a voice that resonated she pleaded with God to forgive them. It was the last thing she said before the man brought the bike lock onto the crown of her head.

"This is what they waaaaaannt!" a voice pleaded from the pack.

45

THE CROWD SURGED FORWARD as Anne fell. Some danced with their hands above their heads, screaming. Others chanted and held their signs up for the cameras. For some though, this was too much. They retreated in horror, looking around for the same police they'd chased away earlier.

A small group in black passed Paul in a dead run, fleeing the scene. Still recording with his phone, Paul saw the bike lock raised and brought down again. Far from shocking the crowd, the horror seemed only to embolden those who remained. They swarmed Anne, and Paul saw legs kicking her, arms swinging with ferocity. And the screams! My God, the screams. Anne wasn't even defending herself anymore.

Anne was being killed.

Paul dropped his bag with his laptop and tossed his phone. He lunged forward, throwing himself into the crowd, knocking over two people in masks on the periphery. He moved forward, turning to the side and edging his way through a swirling nightmare of masks, goggles, and hoodies. He pushed through the crowd, pistoning his legs. Even though he was pushed back, he threw himself forward.

He glimpsed her on the ground, motionless. A gloved hand reached out and grabbed her hair, dragging her a few feet. Her eyes were closed, and her hands trailed alongside her in the dirt. The crowd backed up to allow her to be dragged farther into the graveyard.

Forward. Paul pushed forward. Some in the crowd hit Paul or grabbed him, but it didn't matter. Nothing mattered but getting to Anne. When he broke through to the front of the crowd, he hurled himself into the man standing over Anne, knocking him backward over a gravestone.

"No!" Paul screamed. "No!" He could form no other words, no argument against such horror. "Nooooooooo!" He spun around and saw others behind him dragging Anne by the legs.

He couldn't stop them. There were too many. But he would protect Anne. He threw himself over her, and immediately their blows crashed down on him. Someone kicked and laughed in a high-pitched shriek. Another punched his neck and shoulders while calling him a fascist. Paul wanted to protect his head, but he kept his arms over Anne's head instead. Another blow to his back forced the breath out of his lungs and he could no longer scream. Someone stomped his calf repeatedly.

But Anne?

Anne remained silent.

"Please, please God, save Anne," Paul said as loud as he could. He had nothing to offer God, but he pleaded for her life anyway. "Please, please, God, save Anne."

Something heavy crashed into the back of his head. While his instincts told him to cover up, he continued spreading his arms over Anne's head. *Just stay conscious,* he told himself. *Protect Anne.* The blows landed with increasing frequency, but the pain became more like news of distant tragedies.

When his legs were lifted from behind, pulling him away from Anne, he was shocked back into focus. Paul reached out and grabbed the base of a gravestone. Someone yanked him, and another grabbed his sternum, pulling him off. For a moment he found himself upside down, clinging to the gravestone, his face pressed against the cold stone. Somebody kicked his right arm, loosening his grip, but he held on. Whoever had been holding him up heaved him down next to the white blanket half covered by dirt. Though the pain in his right arm exploded, he reached out and pulled dirt over the white blanket. One arm. Two arms. He finished covering the body. He rolled over, crawled forward, and draped himself over Anne again.

The blows resumed, and just before everything faded into darkness, he thought God had not answered his prayer.

46

Anne Prince changed everything. The entire country witnessed the events of that day on television. Many say it changed them forever. It had to.

Anne had broken the law. No one questioned that. But Anne believed she had to answer to a higher calling. Paul had never believed in callings, higher or otherwise. But that day on the ground, he called out to God. For the first time in his life, he called out in prayer. He pleaded with God to save Anne just as an ambulance pulled in to the rectory parking lot driven by a heavyset twenty-three-year-old rookie EMT with bright orange hair named Donny O'Brien—the same EMT who had responded to Susan Doyle's crisis at the clinic.

Donny had never been a great student or popular in high school. He always shrugged when asked what he wanted to be when he grew up. He wanted to help people. They'd laugh and say that wasn't a job. On the day his father had a heart attack, Donny watched the EMTs work to resuscitate him. An EMT led seventeen-year-old Donny outside the house that day and allowed him to ride along to the hospital in the passenger seat.

After the doctors and nurses resuscitated his father, Donny didn't realize he'd made up his mind about what he wanted to do with the rest of his life, but he had. He had found his calling. He wanted to help people. He'd known it all along.

At St. Stephen the Martyr's Parish, Donny, along with Hardaway and Dougherty, walked past the cameras and delved into the crowd. His EMT partner stayed with the vehicle. Donny asked continually if anyone needed medical attention. When he spotted Anne lying on the ground, he attempted to approach, but the protesters surrounded her and threw stones and branches at Donny and the officers.

They retreated, and on their way back toward the rectory, Officer Hardaway noticed a tall blond man with blood on his shirt sitting against a tree weeping. Michael Olden lay in his lap. Surrounding them, several protesters lay in anguish with broken arms, bruised faces, and lacerations.

"This is the one," Jason said and leaned forward with a grunt, picking up a protester by the hair. "This is the one who hit him with a bat." The man in the mask yelped in pain.

Donny knelt to examine Michael Olden. He checked for a pulse and felt nothing.

"He kept repeating the name 'Claire' over and over again," Jason said, his blond hair streaked with blood. "And then he was gone."

Many camera crews, still unwilling to get too close to the crowd, assembled around the officers and the EMTs asking if police had injured the protesters. They didn't respond.

More EMTs arrived and took the injured away. The blond man had suffered a broken leg and was bleeding internally.

As they lifted Michael onto the stretcher, a skinny man wearing a black do-rag on his head, black sunglasses, and a bandana over his mouth that displayed the teeth and jaw of a skull approached them from the other side of the black iron gate. Dougherty ordered him to step back as they tended to the injured.

"Or what?" the young man, who had thin, pale, white arms asked with a laugh. "What are you and your Nazi comrades gonna do?"

Dougherty stared at him, committing to memory as much as he could about the young man. About 140 pounds, 5 feet eight inches tall. Expensive sneakers. No tattoos. Under his black jacket, he saw a blue shirt with the symbol for the University of Pennsylvania on it.

The masked man turned and spoke directly to the cameras. "The Nazi ideology at its core is founded on violence and on wielding power by any means. The violence these people do against women is the justification for our resistance. Violence as a legitimate tool must be used to combat the creeping threat of religious authoritarianism. At the heart of this debate is the question of whether these people should feel safe organizing as Nazis in public, and I don't think they should. I don't think anyone who is intent on politically organizing for the sake of creating a state-sponsored genocide against women should feel safe. I don't think that's something we should protect. That is something that must be resisted."

"What about free speech?" Jason yelled as he was lifted onto a stretcher.

"Shaming women is not a right," the protestor said. "It's a crime. Using your voice to take away a women's constitutionally guaranteed choice is not free speech; it's violence. And it will be resisted as such." The young man stared into the cameras for dramatic effect. "We will resist you by any means necessary."

The injured were helped or carried to the ambulances. The protesters said they felt unsafe traveling in the same vehicle as Jason.

As the ambulances pulled away, Donny asked the officers if they would accompany him back into the graveyard to check on the wounded. Dougherty looked at Hardaway with a "You believe this guy?" look.

Hardaway got in Donny's face. "Hey, Irish, did you hear that college boy with the mask? They just killed that old man and probably that young girl in there, and he just lectured us about the rightness of his politics. To them, it's 'Punch a Nazi Day,' and everyone but them are Nazis."

"Look, we were ordered not to approach the crowd and wait until Riot Control arrives," Dougherty said. "Any approach is unsafe."

Donny stared at the crowd. There were several competing chants, making them indecipherable, but some of the protesters were sitting, others leaning on gravestones, breathing heavily. The high, raucous, violent energy had ebbed but renewed any time a journalist went to a live shot. Every minute that passed made Anne's survival less likely, so Donny asked the officers again if they would join him in tending to the injured.

"Look, we already have one of ours in the hospital having her face sewn back together," Dougherty said. "We have our orders. We don't go near there until Riot arrives."

"*Your* orders," Donny said. "Not mine." With his medical bag around his shoulder, he walked toward the graveyard.

The two officers looked at each other, sighed, and shook their heads. "A shit show my friend. A total shit show," Dougherty mumbled as the two officers fell in behind the chubby, orange-haired EMT.

Donny tried not to make eye contact with anyone as he walked under the iron archway. The three of them were jostled and threatened by voices deep in the crowd, but Donny kept repeating the same thing: "We're just here to help the wounded. That's all." Both officers scanned the crowd.

One woman wearing a ski mask approached Donny and held out her arm with a scratch that was bleeding slightly. "It, like, totally hurts," she said. Donny rubbed antibiotic cream on the girl's arm and wrapped it in a bandage.

He made his way toward the center of the crowd and saw Anne lying face down in the dirt. Donny crouched beside her, and the crowd circled around him in curiosity. He avoided all eye contact for fear of instigating violence.

He recognized the officer's boots and pants on his left, so he whispered in that direction that they should immobilize her because he feared a spinal injury. Hardaway crouched next to him. "I'm not sure you appreciate the gravity of our situation," he whispered, enunciating every syllable. "Every second we are here puts us and her in further danger."

"I need a stretcher," Donny whispered.

"We got what we got," Hardaway said.

Donny looked to his right toward Officer Dougherty. Dougherty later recounted that moment.

"I'm standing there next to this little fat Irish-looking medic, pressed on all sides by masked assailants. I thought to myself that in twenty-three years on the force, I've never pulled my gun. I didn't think that'd be true for long. I also knew that with so many people around us that if I had to pull my gun, we likely wouldn't survive. The rescue kid didn't see it, but there were two masked guys with knives hidden in their hands within four feet of him and another with a bat behind his leg. And then, get this, this little fat Irish-looking EMT looks up at me and winks. I knew he was up to something. You see, when Irish people lie, there's a glint in their eye. They enjoy it too much, but hey, I was willing to play along because I didn't think I had a prayer of getting us out of there."

Donny stood up amidst the crowd. "She's dead!" he cried. "Anne Prince is dead!"

The shock of it hit everyone. The news passed to the back of the crowd. There were gasps. The cameramen who'd lingered at the fence approached en masse and pushed their way toward the center of the crowd, feasting on the remnants of the event.

As the crowd's attention turned to the news cameras, Donny lifted Anne in his arms. Dougherty and Hardaway glanced at each other. Would the crowd allow them to remove her from the scene?

"Watch their hands," Dougherty mumbled to Hardaway.

Donny hoped the fire had gone out of the crowd with the announcement of Anne's death. One man still voiced violent threats from fifteen feet away, but everyone else was looking around like they were unsure how they ended up there or approached the news cameras to deliver a speech from behind a mask. *Good. Keep your faces in front of those cameras*, Dougherty thought.

He and Hardaway walked backwards, placing themselves between Donny and the crowd the entire way out of the graveyard. In front of the church and separated from the mob, Hardaway and Dougherty lifted Anne into the ambulance, and then Donny drove out with sirens blaring.

47

WITHIN AN HOUR OF arriving at the hospital, doctors placed Anne in an induced coma due to the severe head trauma she'd suffered. She had also suffered several broken ribs, a punctured lung, a fractured tibia, and internal bleeding. Doctors said if she hadn't gotten to the emergency room just then, she would've died. But they were still unsure if she would ever wake and if she did they questioned what level of brain function would remain.

Michael Olden was pronounced dead upon arrival at the hospital. Someone in a black mask had pulled him to the ground. One television camera recorded the attack from just a few feet away. No charges were filed against the attacker because it was determined that Michael Olden died of a heart attack.

The media framed the events of that day as a "violent protest between anti-abortion activists and pro-choice protesters." It remained national news for days. The news that had reported Anne Prince's death corrected their stories. That's when some Christians online called her "the girl who came back to life," but that was never true.

After seventy-two hours, Facebook, YouTube, and other social media giants banned many of the videos of the event, but that seemed to heighten the interest. When questioned, YouTube said they removed the videos due to their graphic nature. They never specified if they were referring to the violence against Anne Prince, the murder of Michael Olden, or the sight of the fetal remains on the walkway.

The fetal remains went missing. A satanic group claimed in a press release to have dug them up and announced they were planning to use them in a sacrifice, but the public outcry caused them to reverse themselves and admit they never actually had the remains. Others said they saw a priest bury the remains in the cemetery in an unmarked grave. Nobody knew for sure.

Paul had suffered a grade two concussion, several sprains, a broken arm, three broken fingers, and internal bruising. He didn't remember the first twenty-four hours after the incident.

Around 6:00 p.m. the following day, Izzy entered his hospital room.

He tensed. He had betrayed her in the worst possible way. He'd used her grief and confusion for his own gain. She'd clearly been crying, and he wanted to comfort her, but she surely hated him. He tried to speak, to say how sorry he was. He wanted to say he was at fault for everything that happened, and he'd ruined her life all for a story, but his voice cracked and he merely exhaled a croaky whisper.

Izzy approached his bedside, her face just above his, and . . . thanked him. "I saw you on television. They were killing her, and you jumped in. You saved my sister. I asked God for help that night, and you, you really were my miracle." She laid her head on his chest and cried. "Thank God for you."

Paul placed his hand on her hair and fell back to sleep.

48

AFTER PAUL WAS DISCHARGED two days later, he and Izzy walked down the hospital hallway together. She had taken his hand in hers when he stood. They pretended she was helping him balance. Neither of them let go.

Anne looked at rest in her hospital room, her head wrapped in bandages, one eye covered, a cast on her arms and stitches on her jaw. But Paul thought she looked at peace. The nurse said they were hoping she would wake soon. Neither Paul nor Izzy asked what it meant if she didn't. They didn't want to hear those words.

The days crawled. Paul stayed with Izzy for most of the day in Anne's room. Izzy's aunts had decided against telling Mrs. Prince anything.

On the third day, a nurse entered the room holding Paul's cellphone in a plastic Ziploc bag. She said the police had found it in the graveyard. Nancy and Robicheaux had called thirty-eight times, but he just turned it off and decided against rejoining the world—at least for a little while. He still felt like his job was to stay with Izzy.

Something about her seemed revelatory to him. No obfuscations, no misleading jokes, no self-protection. She said she had changed that night. She no longer thought about what was owed to her but what she could offer. She laughed that it was actually kind of nice not to be the center of the universe.

At one point a nurse told them it would be good for Anne to hear voices, so they should speak as often as they could in her presence. "That won't be a problem for Izzy," Paul said, smiling.

Izzy hit him in the arm playfully but then quickly apologized, reaching out. "Oh no, did I hurt you?"

"I've had worse beatings," he said.

Over the next two days, Paul told her everything. He held nothing back. He told her about the newspaper, about his parents, about the stories he wrote. He also told her about everything that happened in the church. Every moment he spoke, he expected her to be disgusted by him and walk out. He wouldn't have blamed her. Instead, she held his hand everywhere they went and called him her miracle.

One time Paul was staring blankly at the wall, and Izzy asked what he was thinking. "I think that if all life isn't seen as priceless, it's just a commodity we haggle over, and it's up to each person to decide what's more important than this other person's life. I think that's what we saw in the graveyard. Some people decided that their cause was more important than one life."

Izzy nodded.

"But if God is real, Izzy, that changes everything."

"Everything," Izzy agreed.

Paul called his parents on Izzy's phone just in case they'd seen the news. He left a message for his father. His mother said she always considered the Prince family odd.

One night at around 3:00 a.m., he found himself in the hospital chapel, a nondescript room with symbols of multiple faiths hanging on the wall. And he prayed. He didn't pray for himself. He prayed for Anne and for Izzy. He didn't have words. He could only make a plea, one he wasn't worthy of making, but he prayed anyway. Over the following days, he and Izzy returned to the chapel often.

Six days into Anne's coma, the two walked hand in hand to the cafeteria for lunch. For some reason, Izzy thought the rice pudding tasted great, and every day she'd urge Paul to take a spoonful. He cringed and said it tasted like hospital pudding with BBs in it, but he enjoyed her excitement. She seemed more like her old self again despite everything, or maybe because of it.

That day, exhausted, they fell asleep in the cafeteria, her head on his shoulder. They slept for hours just like that until Paul groggily heard someone turn on the television news about a satellite crashing to Earth somewhere in Florida. Nobody had been hurt, but the town sought to fine NASA for littering.

Izzy woke in a panic. "Oh no. How long were we sleeping?" They ran up the stairs to Anne's room.

The room was empty, and Anne's bed gone.

"Please God, no," Izzy said, fearing the worst. Her hand tightened around his.

They dashed back into the hallway to see a nurse approaching with her hands out in a calming manner. "Anne woke three hours ago. She's doing well. We asked her questions to assess her brain function, and she did great, but she just kept asking if she could be wheeled to Susan Doyle's room. We paged you several times, but you were out, so after the doctors examined her we sent a social worker over to ask Susan if it was OK, given all that's occurred. It turned out she'd been asking to see Anne for days, so we wheeled Anne down."

The nurse stood to the side of the door and pointed them in. Susan, still in a hospital gown, sat on the far edge of Anne's bed. They held each other's hands and wept. "I'm so sorry," Susan said. "I'm so sorry."

"I'm sorry," Anne said.

They looked up as Izzy and Paul entered. Izzy's face contorted, and she stretched her arms out while running to the side of Anne's bed, crying. "I'm so sorry. I'm so sorry. I'm so sorry for everything," she said.

Paul stepped out of the room and into the crowded hallway amid the hurried activities of weary-eyed nurses, orderlies navigating unruly stretchers with wide-eyed patients, and doctors mumbling in quiet conversations with their arms crossed. Since the events at the church, the unremitting and incessant weight of remorse and repentance had weighed on him, and he accepted it as just.

He reached the end of the hallway and turned right and right again until he came back past Susan's door. He looked in, and their three heads still leaned in on one another.

He continued through the hallways, orbiting the Prince family. At some point, he realized he felt light, as if he'd ceased carrying something that he'd long believed part of him. He realized just then that he'd believe for a long time his story was over. Set. But as he walked through that hallway, he was suddenly sure that things were just beginning, that everything so far had been a prequel.

The darkness, anger, jealousy, and rage he'd moved around in his own head like heavy furniture had vanished, and something took its place. Naming it was elusive, but it flooded the empty places, reminding him of something he'd long wanted—needed—to hear.

He was loved.

Once he knew that, he knew what it was he felt : gratitude. It wasn't that he ceased feeling sorry for so much of what he'd done, but he was grateful to be sorry. He was also grateful for the people God had placed in his life, even those he'd failed and who'd failed him. He was grateful most of all for God's insistent grace, which he now knew had been ever present but rejected.

He circled the hallway once more, acclimating himself, and just as he was almost past their door, they called to him.

49

MILTON PRINCE PUT HIS own niece in prison! A six-month sentence!

Yard signs soon popped up all over the state for Milton Prince for state attorney general that read, "Milton Prince: Reform!"

Frank Whipple was still head of the party.

The trucker's strike ended.

Allie Schine resigned from the Blackwell clinic and began work as a realtor to spend more time with her children. Denice Williams received a promotion and believed she might one day work in the national office. The clinic itself, due to the national exposure, received tens of millions of dollars in donations. They built extra rooms.

No charges were filed against the protesters. Many of them wore masks, so it was too difficult to ascertain their identities.

Tyrese and Paul met for lunch at the courthouse just a week after Tyrese had been retired against his will by someone powerful who didn't much like him. "One guess," he said, laughing.

Tyrese pronounced the coffee weak and the bacon soft.

"I hear ya. I hear ya," the young blind woman behind the counter mumbled. "I'll see you soon, Tyrese," she called out when he stood to leave.

"No, I don't think I'll be back," he said. "You've got this, Monica. God bless."

"Oh come on," she said, laughing. "You know you can't stay away from the courthouse."

"Only one court left for me," he said and then limped away, his walking stick hanging idly in his hand. "That's the important one."

Paul didn't know what he meant that day, but Tyrese passed away six weeks later.

Fr. Peter Quinn began working as an administrator in the seminary. He wasn't good at his job, but the seminarians admired him and liked him, so they often covered for him.

Anne Prince lost vision in one eye and continued to suffer headaches. Due to the traumatic nature of her injuries, she needed to learn to walk again. Izzy was there for her every day, holding her up and urging her on. When Anne had recovered sufficiently, she spent three months in prison.

After her early release, Anne and Susan created a crisis pregnancy center just across the street from the Blackwell Clinic. On the wall over a table with a vase of flowers they hung a stenciled sign that said, "God loves you and your unborn child."

Wednesdays and Saturdays were still busy at the Elizabeth Blackwell Clinic. On many of those days, anyone standing at the intersection of Main and Alcorn might see a tall blond man named Jason speaking to anyone who would listen about how his own unborn son had been aborted, and not a day went by when he didn't mourn.

Paul returned to California a few days after Anne woke. Nancy asked him to write a first-person narrative detailing his experience at St. Stephen the Martyr's. She said she wanted it all. So, he wrote about how everything he saw changed how he viewed the world.

When he arrived at work the next day, Nancy invited him into her office and told him there was no way she could run the piece as written. "Look," she said, "this obviously changed you, and I appreciate that, but I'm looking for more of a factual take—"

"You asked for my experience," he said. "I—"

"You know, there's a debate going on in journalistic circles over whether you did the right thing by inserting yourself into the story and protecting that Prince girl. Some say a journalist shouldn't get involved no matter what. Charles wrote an editorial about that. Don't worry. That's the kind of stuff journalism professors love to pontificate about. Should you have gotten involved? I don't know that I would have."

"You know what?" Paul said. "I came here unsure what I was going to say, but—"

"Paul, listen," Nancy said. "Do you know how many 'journalists' come through these doors? My job is to publish a newspaper. Every day. With the Internet now, it's every hour. It's insane. But once in a long great while, a reporter comes in, and they have it. The gift. I mean a real reporter who can smell a story and possesses the gift to communicate it. Look, I don't know if there's a God who gives out talent. But God just gives out the raw materials. My job is much harder. My job is to transform that talent into a skill.

"I can see great things for you here, Paul. Hundreds of reporters come in these doors, and I'm looking for one with the talent, perseverance, and ability to tell a freaking story that explains to people not only what happened but why it matters. That's the real job. It's a calling, actually, much more than job. Who in their right mind would work twenty hours a day seven days a week for crappy pay and a byline? Ninety-five percent of reporters are scribblers who just write down what happened. But the real job? The calling is to make the people out there care. All those people with their bratty children, their sick dog, and mowing their lawns on Saturday must be made to care. And you have that ability. It's rare, Paul. So rare.

"Don't throw it away because some girl caught your eye. Or worse yet, don't throw it away for a cause. Believe me, nothing's more boring than a guy with a cause. People with causes make you write on signs and stand on street corners. Who do you reach with that? Journalists reach millions. That's where the real power is. You think the power is with the politicians? Ha! They're begging us to show up to their press conferences because, here's the truth, if we don't show up, they didn't happen. So, we're not just reporting what happened. We decide what happens. A million things happen every day, but we decide what *the story* is. The narrative. That's power. And all those people in power will bend themselves into pretzels and dance the dance we call. Because we do care. And the people must be made to care."

Paul didn't attempt to interrupt, but Nancy spoke faster, as if he had. "Do you think civil rights just 'happened' in this country? Do you think politicians made that happen? No. It's because we covered the marches. We wrote about Rosa Parks. We poured pictures of the KKK parading down some tiny street in the middle of Bumblecrap, Alabama, into every living room in America. When Americans close their eyes and picture their country, the picture they see in their mind is the one we put there. And the country is better for it.

"So Paul, you can stand on a street corner, or you can help decide which senators and presidents get elected. You can tell people about God and get on your soapbox, or you can be a journalist and affect real change."

Her phone buzzed and she looked down at it. "Oh, I have to take this."

Paul waited until he realized there was nothing holding him there anymore. He thanked her and walked out. He waved to Tom and mouthed the words "Thanks for everything." Robicheaux, on the phone, looked up in confusion and waved.

Outside, Paul blinked in the brightness and smiled.

As he walked through the parking lot, Izzy called his phone. Paul told her they had offered to promote him. He paused. She stopped breathing. "I'll be home by tonight," he said.

She screeched so loudly that he had to pull the phone away from his ear. They talked the entire time he drove to the airport and only stopped when he lost the signal descending into the underground parking garage.

While he walked up the escalator, his phone found a provider again. Izzy had texted him three times. She called him her miracle.

As the plane ascended, Paul opened his laptop. He knew exactly what to write.

CPSIA information can be obtained
at www.ICGtesting.com
Printed in the USA
LVHW081057280121
PP16607600003B/6